# UNLUCKY DIP

## Kate Tenbeth

Front cover illustration
Elizabeth Eisen

Published by Magic Toy Books
ISBN 9780957211988

Kate lives in Essex with her son, who is studying at University, and her two cats, Puzzle and Bud. In January 2011 she helped to set up a writers' group and after hearing one of the guest speakers talk about self-publishing went back home, found some stories she'd written and started the process of learning how to self-publish. She was lucky enough to be signed up by Magic Toy Books in November 2012. She's loved every single second, learnt an incredible amount and is looking forward to writing and publishing many more books!

Elizabeth Eisen is a young freelance illustrator from North London. She graduated from the University of Westminster with a BA Hons in Illustration in 2011 and has since worked on commissions ranging from album artwork to editorial. For further examples of her work go to: www.elizabetheisenillustration.co.uk.

## Dedication

This book is for my son Angus and all his friends – Jon, Max, George (always Moggins to me!), Jordy, Beth, Caitlin, et al.

# UNLUCKY DIP

One minute Holly was leaning against the rails of the riverboat, *The London Pride,* looking at Christmas lights strung out like sparkling jewels along Henley bridge and the next her step-mother, Sylvia, had grabbed her firmly by the ankles and, with surprising strength, had flipped her neatly over the side. Holly's arms and legs tumbled wildly as she hurtled through the damp night air. Her strappy dance shoes flew in different directions and her mobile yet another. She didn't scream, she was too surprised, and she smacked onto the surface of the black water without any semblance of grace whatsoever. It was not something she could possibly have foreseen. It was a raw, overcast evening and up until the whole being flipped into the Thames incident, she'd been celebrating her 15th birthday.

As Holly hit the concrete-like surface of the river the wind was completely knocked out of her and the shock of the ice cold water emptied any remaining air from her lungs. She sank like a stone, her long black hair billowing up around her, but after a few long seconds, her instinct for survival kicked in and she whirled her arms and legs to stop her descent and fought back, frantically clawing her way upwards. As she burst through the surface retching and gasping for lungfuls of bitterly cold air she could just make out the boat tootling happily away from her. Its brightly coloured lights blazed against the night sky, and she could clearly hear the dance music blaring and screams of laughter.

Everyone seemed to be enjoying her party. Jolly good.

A wave from the wake of the boat slapped her face bringing her back to reality. She pushed her sodden hair back and trod water trying desperately not to panic; she looked for all the world like a surprised seal bobbing up and down on the surface of the river. Holly shuddered violently with cold and spat out a mouthful of foul tasting black water. Memories of a school project she'd done on the Thames a couple of years ago flashed like snapshots through her mind and she knew that if the cold didn't get her then there was a good chance the fierce undertow and currents would. The survival rate of being chucked in the Thames wasn't good – there was a lot of history down there that was certainly never going to see the light of day again.

Gulping in shorter breaths now, lips already blue with cold and teeth chattering wildly out of control, she tried to gauge the distance to the bank - it was a lot further than the usual couple of lazy lengths she swam in a heated pool. The sparkling Christmas lights she'd been looking at just before she'd been heaved over the side twinkled encouragingly at her. Damn, Sylvia must have pushed her in at the quietest stretch of water possible but maybe someone walking along the river bank had seen what had happened? Maybe help was on its way right now? She tried to shout for help but all that came out was a gurgle as a passing wave slapped her again and icy air sliced her face, and she knew she'd better get going. Hot tears warmed her frozen skin and her slight body shivered; she couldn't control her chattering teeth nor her tears and she sobbed and shook as she set off unsteadily for the bank.

Sylvia's heart was beating wildly. She flicked back her hair as she leant over the rails of the boat desperately scanning the water for signs of Holly. Please, please let her drown without any complications was the exact thought going through her head.

She bit her bottom lip anxiously, damn she couldn't see properly, the lights from the boat lit up the immediate area around it but the water was churned up and she just couldn't see clearly past a few yards.

# UNLUCKY DIP

She sighed loudly, her beautiful face creased with concern as she considered the situation; the splash was very noisy, surely Holly had been knocked out as she'd hit the surface? If she hadn't been knocked unconscious then the cold would get her. She'd drown either way. God, it had been so much easier killing her father and at least she'd had a body with no pulse in front of her then.

Sylvia turned around and quickly scanned the empty deck. No evidence had been left behind including Holly's mobile which had also gone overboard. She frowned, she needed a drink and she'd better get back before people missed her. She hurried back into the warmth of the noisy, heaving party – she had to be seen by as many people as possible before sending out the frantic warning that Holly had gone missing.

A spasm shuddered through Holly's entire body and her stroke faltered, she was tiring quickly and for every stroke she pushed forward the current seemed to whisk her back three. Her wet clothes clung to her and started to drag her down and gradually her body slowed; her muscles cramped sharply in pain and then became stiff. The bitter cold was winning the battle and the shore and the beckoning lights seemed to blur and be further away than ever.

Holly was only half conscious now, slipping further under the surface with every wavering stroke. She could hear her father's voice softly whispering to her and she wanted to sink down into the comfort of his arms. When he'd been alive he'd always told her diamond days were just ahead but that was just a dream now. The violent shaking stopped and she seemed to freeze like a statue before sliding quietly beneath the waves.

A strong hand firmly grasped the material of Holly's dress, stopping her descent. The first thing that went through Jon's mind as he hung on to her for grim death was damn, for a little thing she was dead weight. Grabbing the back of her dress had been relatively easy, keeping her head above water was difficult, but hauling her up on to the little inflatable dinghy was practically impossible and he was keenly aware that if he wasn't careful he'd end up in the Thames alongside her.

"Hey!" he yelled and shook her as best he could. "Wake up!"

There was no response. Oh crap. He was stuck. The water idly pushed and pulled the girl's body against the side of the dinghy as he desperately wondered what he was going to do next. But then she moved her head slightly. "Grab my hand!" he shouted and reached his free hand towards her as far as he could. A small arm raised itself shakily above the water and grasped it. He smiled, this was better, he had more control now. He inched back slightly and braced himself, one hand still firmly on the back of her dress the other locked onto her right arm. And then he hauled her in, trying to balance her weight against his so that he didn't fall in himself. It took several minutes of strenuous effort but eventually she landed like a fish on the floor of the dinghy and immediately curled up in a tight and very wet ball. Jon took off his jacket and draped it over her, started up the small outboard motor and headed as quickly as he could towards a small jetty.

Holly was oblivious to everything except the extreme cold that seemed to have reached her heart. She'd never be warm again. Tears ran from closed eyes down along ice skin. 'Hold on' she heard her father's voice say and she relaxed, slipping gratefully into oblivion.

# UNLUCKY DIP

## SATURDAY, 17 DECEMBER

Tall, featureless buildings on either side of the road seemed to prop up dark grey clouds that sagged low like overburdened mattresses down into the street. You could smell the rain in the air, damp and heavy, and people scuttled like bugs along the overshadowed pavements anxious to avoid the imminent downpour.

Detective Inspector Ian Drummond flicked through the hastily written reports, drained the last dregs of thick black coffee from a polystyrene cup which he then handed without comment to PC Axler who was sitting in the driving seat of the patrol car. He sighed heavily and rubbed his stubbled chin with the palm of his hand, peering at the same time into the rear view mirror; dark stubble on sallow skin, dark bags under dark brown eyes – might be a good look for some film stars, he thought, but not for him, all-nighters just made him look old and jaded. He smoothed his unruly hair into place and turned to Axler. "So, do you think I pass muster – won't scare her?"

The constable hesitated. Quite frankly, Drummond had a face that would scare the majority of small children even when he hadn't been up all night, and in the cold, grey light of day he reminded PC Axler of one of the older, more hardened criminals they usually locked away, seedy and dishevelled. And that grubby looking old raincoat he always wore didn't exactly help, he looked as if he'd just stepped out of a bad movie... Axler opened his mouth to reply.

"Never mind," sighed Drummond. He vaguely remembered being twenty, knew exactly what was going through Axler's mind and didn't especially want to hear what he had to say. "You stay here, I'll go see her."

"Are you sure you don't want...." But Drummond didn't hear him, he'd already slammed the car door and was making his way to the front entrance of a tastefully refurbished block of 1920s flats. Fat wet blobs of rain started to smack the ground around him just as he got there; he pulled up the collar of his raincoat with one hand while pressing the buzzer to Flat 15 with the other, then craned his neck to look upwards, scanning the apartments quickly. Must cost a pretty penny to buy a flat in this block. More than a policeman's pay. Ah well, he shrugged his shoulders, resigned, that's life and who needed Kensington? No peace and quiet there at all. He stamped his feet to keep warm while he waited. The rain thickened and quickened around him. Come on.

Flat 15 finally answered. "Yes?" came a pleasant female voice.

"Mrs Maddon?      Police, Detective Inspector Drummond."

"Yes, yes, of course, come in." The buzzer sounded, he pushed the heavy door open and walked quickly across the carpeted foyer to the lift. I'd bet anything Axler would already be running up the damn stairs he thought as he waited patiently. The boy probably works out every day. He adjusted his damp raincoat and rubbed his shoes clean on the back of his trousers. He'd been called in just before midnight and it was now midday; he'd worked right through and was dead beat, more than ready to go home but before he could do that he had to speak to Mrs Sylvia Maddon, Holly's stepmother, and update her with what was happening in the search for Holly. She'd left the scene just before he'd arrived so he had no idea what to expect, whether she'd be tearful or composed. He patted his pocket automatically, yes, a small pack of spare tissues was there just in case.

When Sylvia opened the door to him he was instantly aware just how old and tired he actually felt. Forty five years sat like a sack of potatoes on his shoulders, heavy, ungainly, weighing him down. In his line of work he'd come across many mothers and, indeed, stepmothers, of teenagers, but she certainly didn't look like any he'd ever seen before. He guessed she was about thirty; she was wearing light cream jogging trousers and a peach coloured t-shirt that hugged her slim body and she was, without doubt, simply stunning. Straight silky blond hair fell to her shoulders, her eyes were light blue framed by black lashes and her skin was flawless. If she'd been up all night like him she certainly hid it well.

Sylvia Maddon looked at him steadily, her clear blue eyes taking in his appearance without so much as batting a beautiful eyelash. She smiled, her lips red and full, her teeth pure white. "Please come in....?"

"Drummond, Mrs Maddon, Detective Inspector Ian Drummond." He showed her his ID but she didn't even glance at it.

"Oh you poor thing," the red lips pouted sympathetically. "You look so tired, come in, I've just made a fresh pot of coffee, you must have some."

He followed her in to the kitchen. She had a graceful walk, swaying, hypnotic... He shook himself. "I need to speak to you about..."

"Yes, I know, but let's do one thing at a time. I need some coffee to keep me going, I haven't slept a wink you know..." The melodic voice broke, her eyes misted and Drummond felt hopeful for a second that she might throw her arms around him. He suddenly felt uncomfortable, what on earth was the matter with him?

"How do you take your coffee? Hmm, let me guess. Strong and black?" She held up the jug of coffee expectantly and smiled, dazzling him. The four kitchen walls immediately closed in on him and he had a sudden urge for fresh air.

"Yes, yes please. Good guess Mrs Maddon."

"Sylvia, please." Her soft hair fell forward on her face as she leant forward to hand him his coffee.

"Sylvia. Yes, fine. Living room this way?" Drummond turned decisively on his heel and strode out of the kitchen through to the living room and deliberately sat down on a lone dark grey armchair with high, protective arms. He put his coffee carefully on a small table in front of him and looked around taking in the surroundings. The room was sparsely but, he supposed, elegantly furnished, the colours used were mostly black, grey and white – his first impression was that it was like being in an old black and white photo. A single aluminium Christmas tree about half a metre high sat on the dining table but there were no other signs in the room that Christmas was almost upon them - no cards, baubles, Santas, glitter, shopping - nothing. And, he noticed, no photos of Holly. In fact no trace of any teenager. Having two teenagers himself he was surprised. Usually when his kids entered a room, the television remote disappeared into thin air while half-empty crisp packets materialised, usually upside down, on the carpet. Plates of half eaten food slid silently under the sofa and waited, brooding and growing mouldy to be discovered, magazines and books scattered themselves randomly across the floor and sometimes even pictures fell off the wall for no reason. There was nothing like that here. In fact, there was hardly any sign of life at all.

Sylvia sat down smoothly on an adjacent chair and leant towards him, crossing her long legs as she did so. He felt relieved he'd chosen a chair with high, protective arms. "Mrs Maddon... Sylvia..." he began.

She bit her bottom lip with white, even teeth.

"I'm afraid there's still no sign of Holly." His voice was deep and low, meant to be reassuring, yet he hesitated for a second, unconsciously running his fingers through his hair trying to find the right words – words of hope without hope - he'd never yet managed to find them in all the years he'd had to do jobs like this. "This could be for one of two reasons," he continued. "Firstly, she could still be alive somewhere - she may have swum to safety and someone has found her but, I should say if that has happened – if she is safe - she hasn't come forward yet."

He watched Sylvia's reaction as he spoke, ready for the first sign of tears. They didn't come. There was not so much as an intake of breath, no sign of surprise, of grief – nothing. "Or," he spoke carefully, eyebrows raised in anticipation, still waiting for the dam to break, "she may have drowned and her body carried downstream. I can assure you we have search teams, divers looking and they'll continue for as long as humanly possible. There is, however, a chance we may never find her, the Thames doesn't always give up what it's taken." He spoke quickly now, assessing Sylvia Maddon's reaction as he was going. "I'm so sorry to have to tell you this all at once but you have to prepare for the worst. Is there anyone you'd like us to contact, someone who can be with you?"

"So you mean her body may never be found?" Sylvia's face was a mask and he couldn't read her body language at all, but emotion seemed as absent as the signs of Christmas around them.

"I'm afraid there is that possibility." He was unsure of himself now, he was used to dealing with the chaos of feelings like distress, anger and helplessness at times like this but Sylvia seemed anything but upset. Then, for the first time her composure slipped and she looked anxious, her cheeks flushed soft pink and her long fingernails lightly drummed the arm of the settee. "So what does that mean? We can't have a burial? How long will it be before she can be declared dead?"

In an instant Drummond wasn't tired any more, his eyes flickered with sudden interest but Sylvia had glanced away for a second and didn't notice. "Mrs Maddon?" he asked softly.

"Sylvia," she replied automatically.

"Sylvia. Are you alright? I'm sorry if this is a shock. There'll be enough time to go through things like that when you're rested."

She nodded by way of reply.

"Now," he continued getting out a notepad and pen. "I know you've been through all this already, but could you tell me exactly what happened last night? Do you mind me taking notes?" He smiled as he held up the small book.

Sylvia shook her head and frowned, distracted as she thought, her beautifully shaped eyebrows furrowed in concentration. "Well," she said finally. "It was Holly's 15th birthday. We've both had a bad year. Holly's father died earlier this year – a tragic accident while we were on holiday. He fell off the balcony... we were on the fourth floor... we'd only been married a few months..." Her eyes filled with tears for the first time. "I'm so sorry... excuse me..."

"No, no, you take your time," he said in his most reassuring voice giving her a moment to compose herself. While she dabbed her tears he quickly looked around the living room again – not only were there no photographs of Holly, there were none of Mr Maddon either, not even a classic wedding shot.

"She'd taken to being sullen and angry," continued Sylvia. "Especially since we've lived here – we only moved about a month ago from Essex. There's been so much change in her life and she's had such a rough time that I thought it would be nice to get all her old friends together so I hired a riverboat for her birthday and arranged for all of them to be there. And for the first time in weeks she actually looked happy. Teenagers are so hard to please, difficult - you know."

He nodded. Yes, he did know. He had a son back home he couldn't get out of bed and a daughter who only wore black and wanted her nose, lip and any other available extremity pierced.

"Anyway," she continued, "the boat left the dock about eight. There was a lot of music and dancing of course. A couple of the parents stayed so we found a quiet place and just chatted while the youngsters enjoyed themselves. I saw her flit past occasionally but it must have been about 10.30 when I actually went to look for her. I'd got the cake and put in the candles. But when I asked around it turned out that she hadn't been seen for a while."

"Can you be more specific about long she'd been missing?" Drummond's eyes were like lasers now.

Sylvia shrugged her shoulders. "I'm sorry, I don't know – it could have been an hour, half an hour…" She dabbed her eyes with the tissue. "This is my fault," she wailed. "I should have been more watchful, taken more care of her!"

Earlier that morning Drummond had spent a good couple of hours talking to the Captain of *The London Pride*. Together they'd gone over every square inch of the boat; it had been designed to carry people intent on having a good time and that usually meant a lot of drink was consumed so health and safety measures were strictly enforced. The Captain had never before had a single incident where any one of his passengers had fallen overboard and, after having looked around, Drummond believed him. The Captain also informed Drummond that apart from one gin and tonic that Mrs Maddon ordered just after 9.30pm there had been no alcohol consumed on the boat that night – all the guests were under age with the exception of a couple of the parents who stayed on board and none of them touched a drop either because they had to drive home.

And that meant one of two things, either Holly had jumped or - she'd been pushed.

The last thought dropped heavy and unwelcome in his mind; now, where had that come from he pondered, it certainly hadn't been there when he arrived. He rubbed his stubbled chin, deep in thought, the notepad on his lap momentarily forgotten.

Drummond became aware Sylvia was scrutinising him. "Are you alright?" she asked.

"Yes, sorry Mrs Maddon." He sat up straight in the chair and leant forward for his coffee. "Just lack of sleep catching up with me. You say that Holly's father had died recently and that, quite naturally, she was upset." He hesitated before continuing. "I'm sorry to have to ask you this but – do you think she could have jumped?"

Sylvia gazed into space, her beautiful face a blank canvass. "Maybe..." she said slowly. "Holly's mother died when she was eight and she and her father were very close. When I met her father two years ago they were inseparable and I found Holly difficult to handle." Drummond could just imagine. "But she was a good girl, don't get me wrong," Sylvia continued, a tight smile on her lips. "She always got good grades at school and was polite just... distant and difficult sometimes. Her father was her world and she always seemed to resent me no matter how hard I tried, so maybe her taking her own... well, I think it is something that has to be considered."

"You mentioned that you lived in Essex until recently?"

"Yes, in some little backwater." She frowned. "I felt we both needed a change, to get some life, some fresh energy around us so I bought this flat and we moved in just a month ago."

Drummond sipped his coffee and considered. Poor child. Lost her mother, then her father, then dragged away from her home in the country to live in flat in the middle of a city. He wouldn't have blamed her if she had jumped... But did she?

Sylvia uncrossed and crossed her long legs and smiled sweetly at him, flipping her blond hair back from her face. She was certainly good at distraction tactics and he cleared his throat and smiled back while his mind raced. What would she get out of Holly's death? Nothing that was instantly apparent. What was wrong? What was bothering him like an itch he couldn't scratch?

The room fell silent as rain drummed in torrents against the window; in the distance he could hear the muffled sound of a car alarm going off and people arguing.

"Mrs Maddon, are you sure there's no one we can contact? Someone who can perhaps stay with you? I think it would be best if you had someone you could talk to, help you. We may not have news for some time and it could be difficult."

"No, really, I'm fine…" Her voice was suddenly low and tired and she slumped back into her chair, looking vulnerable. He resisted an urge to lean over and pat her hand.

"Well, if you're sure, I'll get back, I'll let you know as soon as we find her…" He stood up, pocketed his notebook, adjusted his crumpled raincoat and started for the door but then stopped. "Oh, I almost forgot," he said. "Do you have any recent photos of Holly I could take with me? Also, could I have a quick look in her room? Sometimes we can see things that parents overlook."

Sylvia nodded briskly. "Of course, I'm sorry, I should have thought about a photo, I'll get one now if you wouldn't mind waiting a moment and then I'll show you her room – not that I think you'll find very much to help – it's jam packed, you know what teenagers are like, won't throw anything away, bits all over the place."

"I know what they're like, I've got two myself, don't worry," he smiled reassuringly. "I'll just wait here while you find the photo - you take your time. If possible a clear head and shoulders shot would be perfect – a recent school photo perhaps?"

As soon as Sylvia left the room Drummond turned and his experienced eyes swiftly took in the room. There wasn't a lot to see. He walked over to the window – sitting on the dining table right next to the aluminium Christmas tree was a small pile of neatly stacked correspondence. The top sheet was a letter from the electricity board. He surreptitiously moved it and quickly read the letter heading underneath. "SHARPE ENTERPRISES" it boldly stated.

Wooden floorboards gave him early warning of Sylvia's imminent arrival back in the room and the top letter was back in place and both of his hands were already in his raincoat pockets when she walked back in the room.

"Here you go," she said. "This is her school photo taken just before the summer holiday."

Drummond looked down at the photo and felt his throat tighten, he'd never got used to kids going missing, maybe dead. He looked into Holly's eyes, grey and intelligent. She had a pretty, heart-shaped face with long black hair and a fringe. She was smiling into the camera. When she was having the photo taken she'd thought she had her whole life ahead of her... He swiftly tucked it into his pocket.

"I will, of course, let you have this back as soon as possible."

"No need," replied Sylvia before quickly adding, "I have lots more, she was such a sweet girl." Her head had dropped slightly as if in remembrance but then she shivered and pulled herself together. "Her bedroom's just down the hall, second on the right. If you don't mind, I'll stay here – I don't think I can go in there just yet..."

Drummond grinned inwardly. Perfect. "Yes, of course, I'm sorry this is so upsetting, I'll be as quick as possible." Before she could change her mind he strode quickly down the corridor. Second on the right...

Slowly and respectfully he opened Holly's bedroom door, reached across to turn on the light and then stepped inside.

Detective Inspector Drummond stood in the doorway of Holly's bedroom. He'd seen many things in his career as a policeman in Central London, the majority of them he had to admit, extremely unpleasant, but he'd never come across anything like the scene before him. It disorientated him and it took him more than a moment to understand what exactly was going on and why.

Uniform brown cardboard boxes standing 4 high lined the walls; even more boxes filled all the available floor space with the exception of two narrow pathways – one led straight ahead to Holly's bed and another, off to the left, led to a desk underneath the window and next to a small wardrobe. School books were open on the desk as if she was going to walk in at any moment and start her homework, and in one corner she'd squeezed a small, artificial Christmas tree decorated with home-made baubles of shiny foil. A small teddy bear wearing a wonky smile and a red waistcoat was propped up against it.

He made his way along the narrow pathway and inspected the cardboard boxes which Holly had draped with fairy lights. They were all neatly labelled in clear, neat handwriting - *Dad's stuff – Holiday - Books/Photos - School Work - Friends*. His jaw tightened in anger and his eyes hardened, Holly's entire life had been boxed and put away – there was no room for it here in London, here in this monochrome flat. On the floor next to her bed was an alarm clock and a photograph that looked worn. He picked it up – there was Holly when she was about five with her parents; she was perched high on her dad's shoulders giggling, her front teeth were missing he noticed. There was a thick carpet of snow on the ground around them and they were wrapped up warm in thick coats, hats and scarves, their cheeks red and glowing. Her mother had her arm around her father's waist and her head was thrown back laughing, her long black hair cascading over her shoulders. Peeping out from her dad's coat pocket was the small teddy that was on now on her desk. As he stood there anger left Drummond to be replaced by immense weariness and sadness.

He heard a slight movement behind him and turned around. Sylvia was leaning elegantly against the door frame, arms folded, a frown on her lovely face. She tsked. "I did tell you it would be difficult to find anything – it's almost impossible to get in here."

Drummond nodded and laid the photo carefully back down on the floor. "Yes, teenagers, all the same. Tell me, please, did Holly have a laptop or a diary or something similar?"

"Why?"

"Well, if she was chatting to her friends on the internet, maybe using Facebook, we may find some clues as to her state of mind. The same for a diary or journal."

"Oh." Sylvia looked surprised, she obviously hadn't thought of that. "Sorry," she shook her head. "She did have a laptop but it's probably still in one of those boxes, she seemed to use her mobile mostly but I suppose she could have a journal somewhere."

"Do you mind if I have a quick look?" He looked enquiringly at her knowing she didn't want him to but had no reason to refuse.

"Of course not," she replied tightly. "Please, go ahead."

"Thank you," he nodded politely and returned to Holly's bed. "Now," he turned and looked over his shoulder at her, "let's see if all teenagers are the same shall we?" He lifted the corner of the mattress and felt underneath. He smiled as he pulled out a journal; the front cover was covered with random drawings and doodles, photos and pictures cut out from magazines. It also had a very solid lock on it. He knew he had very little time, he had to get out of the flat before Sylvia regained her composure and common sense and demanded the journal so he swiftly tucked it into an inside pocket of his raincoat.

"Err, we'll look at this carefully Mrs Maddon, and I'll make sure you get a receipt. And if there's anything that gives us a clue as to why Holly may have disappeared we'll let you know. We'll treat her journal with respect, you have my absolute assurance on that." He was at the entrance of the bedroom now and noted with interest that Sylvia's face was chalk white.

"I..." she held out her hand. Drummond took the proffered hand and shook it. "Well, thank you for your time, Mrs Maddon, I appreciate it. Now you must try to rest, you look worn out. We'll let you know as soon as anything happens." He fished around in the inside of his worn raincoat. "Here's my card. If you have any questions, please call me at any time. Any time at all." Sylvia took the card. Good grief, he noted, even her hands were gorgeous with soft flawless skin and beautifully manicured nails.

"Thank you," Sylvia bowed her head, her soft hair fell forward covering her face. "There's always hope isn't there?" she murmured. "I pray she's found quickly."

Drummond nodded and made his way out, his mind racing; this should have been so simple, so straightforward - go in, see upset and grieving stepmother, offer sympathetic words knowing there was no hope, but saying everything that could be done was being done and that they would keep her fully informed. He'd done it too many times before and each and every time he did it, the experience left a mark, an indelible painful memory on his soul, so he knew without any shadow of a doubt that Sylvia was hiding something. He tried to imagine telling the Chief Super about his instincts but dismissed it almost immediately; knowing something was wrong simply wasn't good enough, he needed evidence, facts. Hopefully he'd find some clues in Holly's diary.

As he went down in the lift he took out Holly's photo and carefully studied her face; she'd fought for survival in a hostile environment, holding onto what she treasured most - her memories. Would she just give in, give up her precious possessions and leave them in Sylvia's hands by jumping off a boat? He pondered the thought - if she was anything like his daughter she'd give any adult a run for his or her money, she'd probably just stay around to be a pain and would enjoy it to boot... Drummond made a spur of the moment decision, he'd been going to leave interviewing Holly's best friend, Georgina, until he'd had some rest but guessed he could nap in the car on the way to Essex; it would take PC Axler a good couple of hours to get there in all this Christmas traffic and, as he strode towards the car, he made a mental note to look up Sharpe Enterprises.

Sylvia watched Drummond from the living room window as he ran across the street through the torrential rain to the patrol car waiting in the layby opposite. He looked up at the window for a split second before he got in and she quickly stepped back. A couple of seconds later she tiptoed back and peered out, the car had gone.

The instant transformation from beautiful to ugly was shocking. Sylvia screwed up her face in anger and swept everything from the table onto the floor in one violent movement, kicking the side of the wall as she did so; she'd have screamed if she'd dared. "Bloody stupid policeman, bloody stupid girl God almighty why on...."

Her mobile phone rang, the shrill sound filling the room. She sucked in her breath, face ashen, it could only be one person. She picked up the mobile and flipped it open gazing blankly at the rain buffeting against the window

"Mark." Her voice was taut and she paced up and down the living room, edgy and restless.

"How did it go?" A deep voice asked. Her heart beat faster. How did it go? She paused for breath and sat down to gain composure. "They haven't found her yet," she replied carefully.

"What does that mean exactly? We don't have much time left."

Sylvia clenched her teeth, like she didn't know that. "I happen to realise that Mark. Funnily enough I'm the one who's been living a lie for over two years, and I happen to be the one who's done all the dirty work so far, or had you forgotten?"

There was a pause on the other end of the phone, she'd never spoken to him like that before and she could almost hear his mind working overtime.

"Sylvia?" He asked in gentle, honeyed tones.

"What?"

"What did the police say?"

She stood up and wandered over to the papers she'd scattered on the floor and picked them up carefully. "The body may not be found. If it isn't found there could be problems about declaring her dead – a slight delay or something...." She put the papers tidily back on the table and then bent to pick up the aluminium tree.

There was a sharp intake of breath. "I thought you'd planned it meticulously, taken everything into account."

Damn it! "Me? *We*, Mark, *we* planned this not just me if you remember." She waved the tree angrily in the air. "Look, she'll be found, her body will be washed up somewhere - they have hundreds of people looking, she's all over the papers and television – it won't take long. We've just got to be patient."

The voice was edgy. "The first of January, Sylvia. The first."

"I know Mark, I know!" She carefully placed the tree in the centre of the table and noted with relief that the surface hadn't been scratched. She felt very alone. Her voice lowered. "Can you come around?" she asked. She could feel tears spring to her eyes and she tapped her front teeth with a fingernail as she waited for a reply.

"No. You know that's not possible." His voice was soft now. "I wish I could, you know that but I can't do anything that would link us. We've played this carefully for over two years, I don't want to lose it by making a mistake now."

She nodded, unable to speak, her heart wrenched open. Another night on her own.

"Sylvia?"

"Yes?"

"Are you okay? Are you going to be able to hold it together?"

Her eyes glazed over. "Yes Mark, yes, I'll hold it together."

"Call me when you hear something."

"Of course."

"We'll meet in a couple of days if she still hasn't been found, I promise."

"Okay."

"I'll call you tomorrow?"

"Tomorrow's fine."

She flipped the phone shut and closed her eyes tightly; she wasn't going to cry. The rain drummed loudly and she opened her eyes and looked around the room - God it was quiet here and she was so tired of being alone. A frown crossed her face, if Holly's body wasn't found soon she'd put on her bloody wellies and go down to the Thames and find her herself – just how hard could it be for goodness sake.

Everything, almost, was going to plan. They were almost there, then no more lying but a wonderful, beautiful life ahead with Mark.

The living room was light, spacious and warm. An old black and white film was on the television giving a low comforting murmur of conversation in the background. A large window gave sweeping views of the Thames and the town of Henley and the sun streamed through it making the tinsel on the richly decorated Christmas tree sparkle and shine. The room had a lived in feel about it; although it was spacious it was also untidy – a couple of empty cans of coke and a half eaten bowl of breakfast cereal were on the carpet waiting to be picked up and taken to the kitchen. DVDs and various games were scattered around the large flat-screen television.

Jon leant forward in the armchair peering anxiously at the girl lying tucked up under a thick duvet on the sofa not quite sure what to do next; he'd hauled her out of the Thames fifteen hours ago and she was still out for the count.

He sat back heavily in the chair and considered his options. The first was to go to the police and let them know that Holly Maddon was lying on his sofa. He'd been keeping an eye on the news all morning, her dramatic and mysterious disappearance was still making the headlines. However, if he went to the police now they would demand to know why he hadn't contacted them as soon as he'd found her. Telling them he wasn't quite sure other than getting her back to the flat and getting her warm had just seemed like a good idea at the time probably wouldn't cut a lot of ice, he'd doubtless end up behind bars accused of kidnapping and reckless endangerment or something like that. It would amuse his mates though.

The second option was to call his dad who was abroad on business at the moment. Jon figured this was an even less viable option, his dad would just go into one, call him stupid and irresponsible and tell him that, as usual, he never thought through the consequences of his actions. Jon sighed heavily, his dad may have a point on this occasion, would certainly never trust him to stay on his own again and would, without doubt, ground him for months.

The third and final option was to leave Holly for a bit longer and see how she did. He cracked his knuckles anxiously – what if she died? What if she contacted some terrible illness from swallowing all that gross water or what if hypothermia had permanently damaged her? Or worse – what if she lived? What if she woke up and screamed blue murder when she saw him? What would he say to her? "Hi, I'm Jon, I hauled you out of the Thames and forgot to tell anyone but no, I'm not really a nutter, honest."

Domino, a large scruffy ginger cat with attitude, rubbed his head against Jon's leg in a desperate attempt for attention. "Wassup Dom?" enquired Jon absent-mindedly. Domino meowed loudly, jumped up onto the arm of the sofa and surveyed the scene. Ah ha, this was new, a duvet had been laid out on the sofa, what a brilliant idea – Jon did love him after all. He strolled over the lumpy bits into the centre where there was particularly good pool of sunshine, settled down and started washing himself. Jon stood up, scratched Dom's ears and headed for the kitchen.

Holly was drifting comfortably, eyes closed, lost in memories. She could hear the sound of the sea in the background and felt the warmth of the sun on her face and smiled; Georgie, her best friend, was lying on a sun lounger next to her. They'd grown up together and knew all each other's secrets but there was one thing that bound their souls together – both of them hated Sylvia.

"Oh my God, she looks better in a bikini than me," Georgie groaned, patting her stomach. "She must be at least 20 years older than me – it's so depressing. And how come her make up never runs? It's not natural!"

"Sssh, she's listening," hissed Holly. Sylvia peered over the top of her novel at them. The loungers were on a white sandy beach. The girls were greasy from sun tan lotion, their arms and backs were gritty with sand and their hair was stiff and tangled from the salt water but Sylvia looked simply elegant, as if she'd just stepped from the pages of a magazine.

"Does she even *sweat*?" asked Georgie.

Holly giggled. "Come on, George, I'll race you to the sea."

"Wow fit or what – at least an eight out of ten?" Georgie pointed openly to a skinny but deeply tanned and handsome boy their own age who happened to be walking by. He blushed deep red, his composure completely blown and scurried past.

"Oh for goodness sake, come on!" Holly grabbed Georgie's arm and pulled her towards the warm blue sea.

When they got back half an hour later laughing and shaking the water from their hair like dogs, Sylvia was waiting for them, her beautiful face calm and composed. "There's been an accident." She took a step forward towards Holly.

Holly took a step back and screamed, the warmth instantly vanished, she woke with a sharp intake of breath and scrabbled to try and find a footing of some kind. She looked wildly around, terrified, disorientated. Something heavy moved on her body and she screamed as a large ginger animal flew past her head.

Jon ran from the kitchen. "No Domino! Bad cat! I'm so sorry! It's okay... please don't scream...." He flapped his hands wildly trying to shush her before the neighbours started knocking the door down. Holly was sitting upright and had squeezed herself tightly into one corner of the sofa, the duvet tucked up under her chin. Her eyes were wild with panic as they zoomed in on him making him stop dead in his tracks. "It's okay, I won't hurt you. I think my cat Domino woke you up." He pointed at Domino who was sitting on the floor washing himself, trying to pretend he hadn't just lost one of his nine lives. Holly looked down at the cat and then back at Jon. She didn't move. Jon ran his fingers through his hair. "Err, look, I'm not going to move this spot until you're happy okay? My name is Jon. Just take a deep breath and have a look around – nothing here's going to hurt you."

Holly frantically tried to gather her thoughts. She stared at the boy in front of her. Tall and skinny, with thick blond hair that was long on top but short on the sides, he seemed to be about the same age as her. His eyes were dark brown and looked rather anxious at the moment. His jeans were ripped and a bit grubby as was his Iron Maiden t-shirt. Iron Maiden? She blinked, confused, who liked Iron Maiden nowadays? Where was she? She gazed around the room; to one side was a window so large it took up almost an entire wall. Outside, dark grey clouds now blocked the sun and the first heavy drops of rain hit the glass. It seemed cold but she was warm, she looked down and noticed for the first time that she was wrapped up in a thick duvet and was on a large settee. She heard the low murmur of conversation and her head whipped round – the television was on in the background. She peeped under the duvet, she was wearing a t-shirt that wasn't hers, her face reddened – her clothes, where were her clothes? She glared at Jon, her grey eyes like flint.

Jon took a step back and swallowed. "I'm sorry," he said nervously. "Please don't scream again, it's alright, honest – you were soaking wet. I'm Jon... sorry, I think I already told you that." He held up a hand and waggled his fingers nervously, he tried to smile but it just made him look more anxious and Holly pulled the duvet tight around her.

There was an uncomfortable silence as they both considered their options. "Err, would you like a hot chocolate?" he suggested out of nowhere. "It's recommended for people recovering from hypothermia you know, I Googled it. You're going to need a ton of calories to get you up and about." Oh my God, thought Jon, cheeks burning with embarrassment, just how nerdy can you get – 'hot chocolate', 'I Googled it', oh my God.

Lost for words Holly nodded slowly and watched him as he ran out of the room. She felt her head sway strangely, it felt heavy. She reached up and carefully patted - what was a towel doing there? She pulled it off and shook her hair eugh, it felt matted and gross.

She surreptitiously sniffed her arm, double eugh, her skin smelt sour and was even more gross. She felt disorientated, very weak and sick and her head swam – probably the smell she thought.

She frowned, her left hand felt tight and painful and she looked down, there was a nasty open gash right across the knuckles but although the edges looked red and sore the wound had been cleaned and she could see dark orange traces of iodine.

She inspected the room she was in more closely; it was open and large, very modern but somehow cosy, just what she'd have chosen with warm, mellow colours, simply furnished but homely and very comfortable. There was a huge Christmas tree – a real one – that must have been about 10 foot high and was heavily laden with richly coloured decorations and candy canes, and sparkled with tinsel and seemingly hundreds of multi-coloured fairy lights. Cards were everywhere, set out neatly on spare surfaces or stuck on walls and any other available surface.

Holly turned her head as the soft murmur of voices faded and was replaced by the harsher and more intrusive music of adverts on the television. Then a pattering sound, low but with a distinct rhythm became louder and more intense and seemed to fill the room – rivers of rain were now racing down the huge window. She watched hypnotised. Black clouds outside, low and threatening filled the Thames from one side to another as if they'd been squeezed from a tube.

The Thames... a chill settled over her as memories, like brief snapshots, started to tumble around her mind then everything slammed back into place and she remembered what had happened.

"What's the time? I need my clothes like now," she called out. "I've got to go home!"

Jon appeared back in the room holding a large tray groaning with food. "Oh, oh right, but I just had a few things ready for you to eat – I thought you might be hungry." He gave an uncertain grin. "That is, if all the water you've swallowed hasn't made you feel ill..."

Holly hesitated, she didn't feel sick but realised she was definitely very hungry. Jon walked over and sat down on the armchair, resting the tray on his lap, his movements were quick and decisive, full of energy.

"Look, I'm really sorry, I didn't mean to scare you," he said. "If it's any consolation, I think you scared me more. Can we start again? I'm Jon McKay." He held out his hand and she tentatively shook it before retreating under the duvet again. "I live here with my father." She looked around but couldn't see anyone else.

"Oh, he's away on business." His speech, like his movement, was quick and energetic. "Won't be back until just before Christmas. My mother hasn't lived with us for years – they got divorced. I have an older sister but she's got her own place so it's just the two of us here."

Holly retreated against the back of the sofa, her eyes wide. Jon realised what he'd said and flushed deep red, flustered. "Oh my God, that was really stupid of me – look what I meant was it's just the two of us but that's okay..."

She raised her eyebrows.

"I mean, I'm not going to hurt you – God, I wouldn't do anything like that." He hesitated, his brown eyes were genuinely concerned. Holly's eyebrows relaxed and she studied him as he tried to reassure her. "Look, you don't have to worry, really. I know this must all seem really strange but honestly, you can just relax while you're here, I won't hurt you and you can leave any time you want. I pulled you out of the Thames last night – you seemed to have fallen in... can you remember anything?"

Oh yes, Holly thought, I remember everything, and her eyes glittered in anger. Jon hesitated briefly as he caught the look and hoped it wasn't directed at him. "You were pretty out of it last night but I kept you as warm as possible and now, well, I'm not an expert but I think you just need some food to build you up and a bath. And you may feel a bit sick – who knows what you swallowed but you can stay here as long as you need, there's no rush, it's cool."

Domino stood up, tail twitching wildly and meowed loudly. Jon visibly relaxed and smiled widely and Holly noticed he had a nice smile when he wasn't nervous. "Oh, and this is Domino. He's called Domino because his favourite food is pizza." He absent-mindedly scratched one of Domino's ears and a rough purring started up. "Don't think I don't know you're eye-balling the food – none for you." He quickly scooped up the cat and put him firmly away from the tray. Domino, betrayed to the core, immediately stopped purring and glared accusingly up at him.

Jon straightened a plate on the tray and smiled encouragingly. Holly felt herself relax a little, maybe she should get some food in her and have a shower before she sorted out Sylvia, she'd need all the strength she could muster.

"Well, okay, thanks – I'm Holly..." She looked at the tray of food still sitting on his lap and her stomach growled. Was he going to keep that tray there forever?

"Ah yes, yes, I know who you are. Look, you eat first and we can talk after. Cool name Holly by the way."

"It was my birthday yesterday...."

"Ah. Well I guess saying belated happy birthday might not be appropriate considering what you've been through. But I'm guessing you're called Holly because you were born so close to Christmas – right?"

"My parents met at Christmas in a garden centre – they both reached out to pick up the same bunch of holly." Holly's face fell and she looked bereft, vulnerable.

"I'm sorry," Jon said gently. "Look, I won't talk any more, I think you should just eat, you've been through a heck of a lot." He sniffed and coughed. "And then, I don't wish to be rude but I think you need to shower."

Holly blushed deeply and pulled the duvet up further around her. "I'm sorry I'm pretty gross aren't I?" she said miserably.

"No!" he countered quickly. "Sorry, I didn't mean it quite like that, you don't smell that bad – hey, you haven't been near my room yet!" Jon grinned widely. There was an awkward silence.

"Hmm," she said quietly. "Thanks for helping me."

Jon placed the tray on the coffee table just in front of the settee then stirred and handed her a mug of hot chocolate in one swift movement. Even though he was obviously trying to slow down for her sake he was just an intense ball of energy and she wondered if he was like that all the time or if it was just because he was nervous.

"It's not too hot, so you don't have to worry about burning yourself," he assured her. "Just get it down. Now, apparently you need a high calorie intake, so okay what are you up for?" He pointed at the groaning tray. " – pancakes, toast, porridge? Porridge would be good? You just go for it."

A shaky arm appeared from under the duvet and pointed to a plate stacked with pancakes. "Cool," he commented. "They're my favourite too," and poured almost a whole jug of maple syrup over the top before handing the plate to her. Domino meowed loudly and stretched up to see what she'd chosen.

The first mouthful was delicious and although she started eating slowly she soon picked up speed and quickly demolished the pancakes before starting on the porridge. As she handed the bowl back Jon quickly handed her some toast he'd just buttered. "Wow, well swallowing half the Thames doesn't seem to have done you any harm!"

Holly stopped, heavily laden toast and marmalade half way to her mouth and looked at him, unsure. Jon noticed that her eyes, framed against her black fringe and pale skin, were huge and a fantastic grey colour like a dark sea on a stormy day.

"I'm sorry," he faltered. "You know I didn't mean that as it came out...."

She grinned, feeling a lot better already. "No, no don't worry, no offence taken – it's really nice of you to go to so much trouble, you're a brilliant cook you know. I just feel as if I haven't eaten for a week. And thanks, thanks - I'm really feeling a lot better." The toast made its way into her mouth and then she carefully inched herself forward on the sofa, gathering up the duvet around her. "And now I have to leave," she stated firmly.

As she stood up her legs gave way but Jon was there instantly, supporting her and gently sat her back down. She frowned, angry with herself for not even being able to stand upright. "Well, I guess I'm not going anywhere right at this moment. But I can't stay, I've got to go..."

"Yeah, I know, when I first got you back here you were shouting about killing someone and I guess you've got to go and sort them out but really you know you'd be wise to try and build up your strength first. Also, you've still got to have a shower and you haven't got any money or clothes – I washed what you were wearing, everything's clean and dry, but I honestly don't think you'll be able to use them again."

The enormity of the situation hit Holly and she ducked her head down so he couldn't see she was upset. Of course she had no money, no shoes even, what about her mobile? She couldn't go home, could she? Sylvia.... Sylvia would make out it was her fault and maybe try to murder her again. Maybe Georgie could help? She bit her bottom lip anxiously as she thought.

Jon watched the many emotions cross her face closely; he gently cleared his throat as he waited for her. Holly looked up, her jaw set firm. "Thanks, if it's not a problem I'd like to stay for a short while if you don't mind. I've just got to think about what I'm going to do – it's a bit of a tricky situation. But I've got to leave as soon as possible."

"Look," Jon spoke quietly. "There's something you should know - your disappearance has been all over the television. I wasn't sure whether to show you just yet, but I guess there'll never be a perfect time." He reached across the coffee table, picked up a remote control and flicked a button, the black and white film snapped off and bright coloured images immediately appeared and sound filled the room. "I recorded this from last night's news," he said.

Holly found herself staring at Sylvia. She appeared to be standing near to *The London Pride*, it was night but bright lights blazed and she was being jostled and microphones were being shoved at her. "What do you think happened to Holly?" asked one female reporter.

There was a close up of Sylvia's face. Perfectly made up as usual Holly noted and scowled. Moist tears appeared in Sylvia's eyes and she flicked back her blond hair to give the camera a clearer view of her face, "I don't know," she sniffed. "We noticed she was missing on the way back... I went out to find her because we had her birthday cake and we were going to sing happy birthday to her..." She broke off and her face crumpled. Someone patted her arm reassuringly. "It was her birthday, her fifteenth... but she lost her father just a few months ago... maybe... maybe she just couldn't manage without him...."

"Are you saying this may not be a tragic accident but that she may have killed herself?" asked another reporter not quite as sensitive as the first.

Sylvia looked skywards, her chin trembled, "I don't know, I just don't know... but I'm going to stay here as long as it takes, until they find her."

A policeman interrupted. "That's enough now. Mrs Maddon needs some privacy. We'll take it from here."

A microphone was immediately shoved under his nose. "And what exactly are the police doing about this?" demanded a reporter.

There was the sound of an engine starting up behind them. "Well, as you can see, we're working with the London Coastguard and have all available boats out. They'll keep searching up and down the route the pleasure boat took and further downstream. We'll do whatever it takes to find Holly."

"But it's freezing. What are the chances of her surviving the night in the water?"

The policeman looked uncomfortable. "I can assure you that we are doing everything possible to look for her."

The cameras turned their attention to a group of youngsters in the background, all pale and shocked, sitting huddled on a low wall. Adults fussed around them. Holly could clearly see Georgie looking lost and crying, wandering away from the others, silver foil blanket around her shoulders, and she held out her hand to the screen as if to touch her. "Oh Georgie," she said sadly and hot tears spilt down her face.

Jon turned off the television and turned to Holly, his face sombre. "I'm really sorry," he said quietly. "Are you okay? I know this is a lot to take in. I should have gone to the police I guess, but everything happened at once and I was so busy making sure you were dry and warm that time flew by, then I thought it best not to tell anyone you were okay until you woke up. Are you alright?"

Holly nodded miserably, her mind reeled with images, memories and she was angry beyond comprehension. She lay back on the sofa and closed her eyes, thinking.

Jon looked anxiously at her, she was even paler than before if that was at all possible and the charcoal smudges under her eyes seemed to deepen as he watched. Dark clouds filled the sky outside and seemed to close in on the room.

Then, abruptly, she sat up startling him. Domino jumped an inch off the carpet. "She tried to kill me, I swear she did! I was leaning against the rails of the boat getting some fresh air and she came up behind me, she dropped her keys or something I think, bent down pretending to pick them up, grabbed my ankles and tossed - just tossed me like a freakin caber overboard! And now she's saying I killed myself. I don't believe it! And I'm damn sure she killed my dad!" She grabbed the duvet again. "Just let me get her – or I'll go to the press, I'll tell those reporters a thing or two."

She got as far as the coffee table this time before her legs gave out. Jon neatly caught her again and sat her down. She kicked the side of the sofa angrily as she tried to catch her breath. "I am just so going to get her!"

Jon sat down next to her, stunned. "Really? She tried to *kill* you? *And* your father?" He paused as he tried to take in the enormity of the situation; in his mind's eye he could clearly see his own father, hands on hips, telling him to think about the consequences of his actions and instantly dismissed the vision. His brain took a quantum leap forward. "Well, look, I'll help you, it's not a problem, honest."

"Oh really? And what exactly do you think you can do to help? Did you just hear what I said? She tried to kill me!"

Jon flinched but said nothing and they sat quietly side by side for a minute.

"I'm sorry," said Holly.

Jon shrugged and held his palms up. "Hey, extenuating circumstances and all that."

Holly nodded. "Look, thanks but I don't think you should get involved, this is real - I mean she's already killed once – at least I think she has – and she definitely tried to kill me... You could get hurt, she's got to be psychotic or something and who knows what she'll do."

"The chances are I'm already in a load of trouble, and honestly, I really do think I can help you..." persisted Jon.

"How?"

"Well, I'm a genius with the computer for one thing, I can find out all kinds of stuff."

Holly cast a sideways glance at him - had he even registered she'd said that Sylvia was a killer? That this wasn't a game? She blew out a big sigh, but then what did she know about dealing with a killer?

Jon sensed she was weakening. "We can be in this together, you do need some help don't you? Two heads are better than one and we can plan properly..."

"I just don't think it's a good idea."

"We don't have to go near her, we can do it all on line."

"Really?" Holly looked doubtful.

"Really. Look, at least give me a chance to show you what I can do."

"You won't get hurt or killed or anything?"

"I seriously wasn't planning on it," replied Jon.

Holly frowned and then held out a hand. "We'll work together then."

Jon shook the proffered hand enthusiastically. "Deal!" And although Domino hadn't taken his eyes off the tray of food for a second he also gave a heartfelt meow – they were all in this together.

Night had already closed in and Jon pulled the curtains, shutting out the oppressive dark clouds which were still low in the sky. The living room was warm and cosy and he went into the kitchen to prepare supper, noisily clattering pots and pans and singing cheerfully at the top of his voice. Domino was curled up tightly on the settee snoring into his tail, the Christmas tree lights sparkled and although the news was on the television the sound had been turned down low so it was only a quiet murmur in the background. Holly had showered and change. She'd already found the cutlery and had put it on the coffee table along with some glasses and paper napkins and was standing at a long sideboard reading some of the many Christmas cards on display. She was feeling a lot better now she'd showered and had clean clothes on.

It turned out that Jon's older sister, Alex, sometimes stayed over and had left a few odd bits of clothes and although she was a little taller and perhaps a size bigger, her taste wasn't bad at all. Jon told Holly she could borrow whatever she wanted, apparently Alex wouldn't notice if some of her clothes were missing. Thank goodness, thought Holly as she preened in front of the bedroom mirror. And, she'd noted smugly, when she'd first reappeared in the living room, it had been Jon's turn to do a double take. Her black hair had been blow-dried and fell thick and shiny almost to her waist. Colour had come back into her face but even the dark smudges that were still there under her eyes merely accentuated their gorgeous grey colour. She'd picked out jeans and a pink crop top and they fitted her perfectly.

Jon had taken a deep breath and looked around for help but only Domino was in the room and he wasn't exactly forthcoming. "Wow," he eventually said. "You smell a lot better." As the words left his lips he rolled his eyes, why on earth had he said something that awful? "You know, I didn't exactly mean that as..." He ran his fingers through his hair in desperation, his face stricken.

"Yeah, I know," replied Holly swiftly. "You didn't mean it as it came out. No offence taken at all, you're right – even I know I smell a hundred percent better than I did before!"

It had been a long and laborious business of getting rid of the stench of the Thames. Holly had had to wash her hair three times and then she'd scrubbed herself almost raw to remove the sour odour from her skin. As she'd showered her anger had disappeared and helplessness had almost overwhelmed her; the depth of Sylvia's action was so deep and black Holly thought she would fall forever downwards and never find her way back if she let herself think about it. Her face crumpled in pain, her shoulders shook and hot tears ran fast and furious down her cheeks. She'd leant both hands against the tiled wall and bowed her head forward between her outstretched arms, eyes closed. Fierce jets of hot water hit the back of her neck and then ran in torrents down her slim back.

Scenes from the previous night tumbled and flashed through her mind, bright, colourful and magnified a thousand times. She just wanted to sit in the corner of the shower and make herself as small as possible but she wouldn't, she remained standing while the water streamed over her. She wept tears of despair for her father, for Sylvia's betrayal and for the cold breath of death she'd felt whispering to her and then, after an endless time, she lifted her face to the pounding water and let all her tears be washed away.

Anger once again reared its head and replaced fear and helplessness and this time it settled in, cold, calculating and unforgiving.

"Food's just about ready!" Jon called through from the kitchen disturbing her thoughts. "Everything okay in there?"

Holly was still standing at the sideboard gazing blankly at the Christmas card in her hand. "Yep, no problem," she shouted back. Domino briskly opened his eyes, food was on the way.

Jon appeared in the doorway, a big smile on his face and a plate of gently steaming spaghetti carbonara in each hand. The smell was gorgeous and filled the room. "Voilà! Food is served, please take your seat madam."

Holly smiled and sat next to Domino on the settee and Jon handed her a plate piled high with pasta.

"Like wow," she said impressed. "Am I meant to eat all that?"

"Hey, you still need tons of calories," he explained. "Hang on a minute, I'll just go get the ciabatta."

When he returned Domino was sitting up and staring fixedly at Holly. "You behave," Jon instructed sternly. "Freshly prepared cat food full of the correct amount of vitamins and minerals for a cat of your mature age is in the bowl on the floor in the kitchen, which is where you should be at this moment in time." Domino didn't even blink and Holly wondered if he always talked to his cat like that – Jon was really nice but definitely quirky – her dad would have liked him she thought.

He sat down on the armchair next to the settee and reached for the plate of pasta waiting on the coffee table. "I'm so ready for this. Have you had enough of the news? We can watch something else if you like and catch the local news at nine, check if there's an update?"

"Yeah, that's fine, I'm fed up of seeing Sylvia crying anyway," replied Holly. "What about some music?"

He flicked through the channels until he found something they both liked and then they settled back, comfortable in each other's company.

"This is really good," said Holly munching her way through with great enthusiasm. "You're a great cook you know, way better than me, I burn everything. Been trying to cook since I was eight but never got the hang of it and dad always did the meals..."

Jon grinned. "Thanks, well they do say the best chefs are men..."

Holly rolled her eyes.

"Just saying..." said Jon. "Er, do you think you're up to telling me how you got tossed like a "freakin caber" into the Thames?"

"Yep," she nodded firmly and tore off a bit of ciabatta chewing it slowly wondering how exactly she was going to tell him about her life, the right words weren't easy. She decided to start from the beginning, telling him briefly about the death of her mother when she was eight and the impact that had on her life. She explained how, despite everything, she and her dad had coped. "He was an architect," she explained, "and when mum died he stopped working in London and set up his office at home so we could be together more. He made me breakfast every morning, and nagged me about homework, even made my costumes for school plays – badly, but he did try - he was fantastic, you'd have loved him..." She tailed off and pushed the remaining pasta around her plate with her fork. Jon waited patiently for her to continue, he could see how hard it was for her to talk about her father.

"And you know he never really seemed that interested in meeting anyone else although trust me, some of the mums made really heavy plays for him, I mean he was tall and good looking, but then one day a couple of years ago he'd started dropping the word 'Sylvia' into conversation. I was stupid really," she sighed, "I completely missed the clues until out of the blue one day he asked if I'd mind meeting someone he thought was special? Special? Hah!" Holly scowled. "Poor dad didn't stand a chance – well, you've seen her! She's beautiful, just stunning – no one can see past it, it's like she mesmerises them."

Jon nodded but didn't comment, he may only have been 16 but he knew better than agree with the fact that Sylvia was beautiful.

"Dad really loved her!" continued Holly angrily. "What could I do? I didn't want to see him unhappy and he'd been through so much already. They married less than a year later and no, I was not a bridesmaid, no way you'd catch me in a frilly dress."

"What happened after they were married?"

"Within a few weeks she had him back commuting to the City and I didn't see him any more – he was gone before breakfast and got back so late he was too tired to talk properly. Really, he was way too old to start commuting but she wanted lots of money. He started to look ill, he got dark circles under his eyes..."

"Did she work?" asked Jon.

"Sylvia work? Yeah, well, in theory she did. Each day she drove couple of miles into a solicitor's office in Chelmsford where she answered the telephone and complained a lot. That's all she ever seemed to do, complain. I spent most of my time upstairs in my room or with Georgie – the one on TV who was crying.

"And then in August we all went on holiday together to Barbados. Dad said I could take Georgie with me for company which made it bearable. And, you know, I never told anyone except Georgie that I hated her. I didn't think anyone else would believe me, they'd just have thought I was jealous, she's so beautiful."

Her voice fell to a whisper as she told him about her father's death in Barbados. "But was it an accident?" she turned to him, her grey eyes stormy. "I don't think so, but then why would she kill him? He loved her, adored her and she had everything she wanted... She inherited everything but it wasn't as if he was a millionaire or anything... And why try to kill me – I don't have anything! Why tell people I was suicidal? Suicidal for goodness sake! I wanted to be an architect like dad, to make him proud of me. I wasn't happy living with her but I was coping, just waiting really until I was old enough to leave..."

Her fingers angrily drummed the arm of the settee as she continued. "She sold our home in Essex just last month. I've got nothing now – all my friends, people I've known all my life – everyone – I had to leave everything. We moved into a flat in Kensington – apparently there's more life, 'more energy' in London."

She paused for a second while she pushed the curtain of hair back from her face. "I can't see the sky from my bedroom window and there are so many people, I hate it. But," she continued, her face a mixture of anger and resentment, her voice rising, "here I am. What do I do now? Where do I go? I can't go to the police, they'll just hand me over to her and she could try to kill me again – no one will believe she tipped me out of the boat, they'll think I'm just making it up... I'm a teenager, everyone thinks we're hormonal and out of control, they'll put me in a home..."

Jon was quiet, his face grim as he listened carefully. He didn't know how to reply, in comparison his life had been incredibly easy and uncomplicated. Yes, his parents were divorced but even that had been amicable. He shook his head, he wanted to reach out and hug her, to make everything better but knew that if he was going to help her he had to think logically. "That's an awful lot to take in," he finally replied, choosing his words carefully, "and honestly Holly I don't know how you've coped, but the bottom line is we've got to be practical and sort out a plan so you can be safe."

Holly swallowed, sucked in a deep breath and nodded silently by way of reply. She stood up and headed towards the kitchen. "I need to get some more coke – d'you want some?" she asked.

"Yes please." He didn't follow her, he instinctively knew she needed a couple of minutes to herself. Domino meanwhile had no intention of going anywhere until the pasta situation was sorted and while he waited he started the massive job of grooming himself, beginning with his ears and purring loudly as he progressed. Jon peered at him. "Can you keep it down, every other cat manages to clean themselves without making a racket, I need to think." Domino didn't raise an eyebrow or miss a beat but continued diligently with his work. Holly returned from the kitchen and handed Jon a can of coke. "Thanks," he said automatically.

She plumped down on the settee next to him and stroked Domino. "I'm sorry I got upset," she said quietly, "and there's something else I need to say - thanks, you've been really cool about taking care of me and especially not telling the police I'm here - I'm really pleased you're the one who found me." She held up her hands and examined them, the gash across the knuckles of her left hand still looked raw and she winced as she tried to make a fist. "It hurts," she noted, "but that's okay, I'm alive, and you're right, we need a plan, I'm going to be practical like you said and find out what happened to my dad and why Sylvia tried to kill me."

"I can help you do that," said Jon. "I know this isn't a game Holly, I'll help you find the answers and make sure you're safe from her for good, I promise. We'll start work now - if we're going to prove to the police that Sylvia tried to kill you and that she may even have killed your dad, you need to tell me everything you can remember – names, where she worked, what she did before she met your dad – *everything*. We'll have to do a lot of background research, and you've struck lucky, you've come across a genuine computer nerd - there's not a lot I can't find out when I put my mind to it."

"You won't get into trouble will you?"

Jon considered, he was already way past the point of being grounded. "Not a problem, seriously, we just need to approach the problem from a point of logic, break it down one thing at a time." His eyes were serious and his energetic body momentarily calm as he focussed on the task ahead. "We can do this, I know we can."

"When does your dad get back?"

"Christmas Eve."

"That's not long."

"You're right but then again it could be long enough... we just don't know."

Holly scratched Domino's ears while she considered. Memories of scrambling desperately through the water almost overwhelmed her and she felt her anger return. "Yeah, you know something Jon, you're right, it could be long enough and we *will* find out the truth. More than anything else I need to find out if Sylvia killed my dad and I'll do whatever it takes."

"Whatever it takes?"

"Yep." Holly's chin was firm and she brushed her hair back over her shoulder.

"Well okay then, let's get going!" said Jon. "Oh, and by the way, while I'm on the laptop can you do the dishes..."

Holly coughed and wilted visibly.

"Whatever it takes you said..." Jon stood his ground

"Yeah, yeah, I'm on it..." she picked up a couple of glasses and headed for the kitchen. "Just like a guy..."

PC Axler pulled up outside Georgie's home in Little Hambleton, Essex. They'd been held up for hours on the A12 due to an accident, not that Drummond had noticed because as soon as he'd settled in the back seat he'd pulled his raincoat around him and slept the entire journey. When the snoring had first started Axler had raised his eyebrows and smirked but after the first ten minutes the amusing side had well and truly worn off and he'd never been so relieved to arrive at a destination in his entire life.

He got out and stretched before stepping around to the back of the car. He looked through the window at Drummond who was still fast asleep; his mouth was slightly open and he'd taken his seat belt off so he could put his feet up on the back seat. He reminded Axler of a bag of groceries that had been thrown haphazardly into the car and it was hard to believe his reputation at the station, he looked as though he didn't know where he was or who he was half the time. According to rumour he'd been headed right for the top but wouldn't conform to rules and regs, had been a Detective Inspector for years and always would be.

Axler shrugged his shoulders and breathed in the cool night air. He hesitated as he put his hand on the car door handle and gave a slight smile - if he opened it quickly enough the old man would fall out in a heap. As he stood weighing up the pros and cons of such an action he became aware he was being scrutinised. "Problem Axler?" came a deep voice.

"Err, not at all Sir. Sorry Sir. We're here." He opened the door politely and out stepped Drummond adjusting his tatty mac. The stubble on his chin seemed to have grown by a good half inch during the journey.

Drummond looked at the house where Mrs Langstone lived. It was an ordinary semi-detached house with a wonky path leading to a dark green door that had a huge and untidy Christmas wreath on it. Wobbly fairy lights, twinkling brightly, framed the windows and he could hear the faint sound of 'Rockin Around The Christmas Tree' coming from inside.

"Hmmm. Axler, you can come with me this time." And with that he opened the gate and strode up the garden path.

He rang the doorbell. The music was immediately turned off. He could clearly hear an excited yipping noise and a, "Oh heck – will you... oh good grief!" and then the door opened. Mrs Langstone stood there, she looked from one to the other but her sights homed in on Axler's uniform. Her face paled and tears started to roll down her face. "Oh my God, you've found her! She's dead! Please tell me she's okay!" Her shoulders shook, her face crumpled and she stood on the front door step sobbing. "I'm sorry, I'm sorry," she tried to control herself and she dabbed her tears with the tea towel she was holding. A Labrador puppy pushed his way through and barrelled out onto the path, fat and honey coloured, his entire body wriggling from nose to tail.

Drummond bent down, neatly picked him up and handed him to Axler. "Here you look after the pup." The puppy was delighted and wriggled and licked Axler's nose and chin. PC Axler had a big grin on his face as he held the pup tight – a meeting of minds thought Drummond wryly. He turned to Mrs Langstone. "Is it alright if we come in for a few minutes?"

Mrs Langstone peered out from behind her tea towel, her face blotched, her eyes red and raw – she'd obviously been crying a lot. She was quite short with dark curly hair that framed her plump face. "Yes, yes, sorry, I'm so sorry, please do come in."

The hallway was crammed with coats and shoes, unopened cards, tinsel and other miscellaneous Christmas items. "Oh mind the..." she pointed to a puddle on the carpet. "He gets excited when the front door bell rings..." Drummond smiled. This was more like it – chaos – this he could cope with.

"Mum? Mum!" came a shout from the top of the stairs.

Mrs Langstone's face was ashen as she looked at Drummond. "Georgie," she said. "I... we were up all last night, I thought she'd finally got to sleep..."

"I'm sorry for disturbing you both, Mrs Langstone."

"Oh no, I didn't mean..." she looked distressed.

Drummond spoke loudly. "Georgie, it's alright, nothing to worry about, I'm a policeman and I'm here to see you and your mum about Holly. If you'd like to come down I'd be very pleased to talk to you."

A high pitched scream came from the top of the stairs and Mrs Langstone raced up. PC Axler raised his eyebrows and tried to contain the wriggling puppy. "Well, that went well Sir".

Drummond gave a deep sigh. He spotted the kitchen ahead. "I'll put the kettle on Mrs Langstone," he shouted up the stairs. "You and Georgie come down when you're ready. Axler, find the front room please and see if you can calm that dog down." The puppy yipped and licked Axler's chin.

The kitchen looked like an explosion had taken place - cake mixture was still in a large bowl, carrier bags were half unpacked and the sink was full of dishes. He found the kettle, filled it with water and put it on. He opened a few cupboard doors, found some mugs and tea bags and stood there feeling quite comfortable as he waited for the kettle to boil.

Mrs Langstone appeared. "She's just putting on some clothes, she'll be down in a minute." She looked around the kitchen. "I'm so sorry about the mess, it's not usually as bad as this. I just don't seem to be able to concentrate..." her eyes filled with tears again.

"Just like my own house, don't worry," said Drummond knowing his wife would kill him if she heard him say that. "Now, how do you take your tea?"

"A couple of spoons of sugar please," she replied. "And the same for Georgie. What about the young constable?"

From the front room Drummond could hear, "Who's a gorgeous boy then? Who's a gorgeous boy?" There was the sound of yipping in reply and Drummond raised his eyebrows. "He'll have two spoons as well."

"Mince pie?" Mrs Langstone was nervously piling mince pies on to a plate, her hands were shaking.

"Yes please," said Drummond. "They look wonderful – did you make them yourself?"

She nodded miserably and took the plate into the front room. There was a loud clatter down the stairs – Georgie was on her way. "Oh heck! He's done it again mum – you could have warned me, my sock's soaking wet now!" She appeared in the kitchen doorway holding a single sock in one hand, the spitting image of her mother, short and slightly plump with dark curly hair.

"It's Holly isn't it?" she demanded. "Have you found her? Where is she? Is she okay?" Her dark brown eyes were like saucers, her face pale.

Drummond handed her a mug of tea. "For your mum. Let's go into the front room and talk shall we?"

The front room was cosy and dominated by a large tree that seemed to have been rather randomly decorated – there was nothing at all on the bottom branches at all he noted, everything seemed to have been crammed onto the top half. Ah... the dog. Drummond looked over at PC Axler who was kneeling on the carpet in the midst of a tug of war game, the puppy was growling and shaking a piece of silver wrapping ribbon from side to side – it was obviously a very dangerous piece of ribbon.

"Axler," said Drummond.

"Sir." Axler stood up. The silver ribbon fell to the carpet.

"Sit down Axler - on a chair, please. Mrs Langstone, Georgie," he pointed to the sofa. "If you wouldn't mind, I just need to speak to you, get a few details." He sensed a welling of tears but Georgie and her mum managed to compose themselves and sat quietly down as they'd been asked on the sofa. He pulled up a chair and sipped his tea.

"I'm Detective Inspector Drummond, Mrs Langstone. This is PC Axler." Axler sat straight holding his tea and trying to ignore the puppy now chewing his shoe laces.

Drummond's face was calm as he looked at the two women, so different from Sylvia he thought. "Firstly," he said as gently as possible, "I'm here to tell you that, I'm sorry, we still have no news about Holly."

"But that's good isn't it?" asked Mrs Langstone anxiously, holding firmly onto Georgie's hand. "It means she's not... dead?"

Drummond hesitated, this was never easy. "Well, I'm afraid no, not necessarily," he looked from fearful face to fearful face. "I'm sorry, I can't promise you that everything will be alright, that Holly will be found alive and well - the London Coastguard were on full alert immediately they were informed and are still literally scouring the river looking for her but I'm afraid there's no trace so far."

"What are the chances of her surviving?" asked Georgie bluntly.

Drummond looked at Mrs Langstone, trying to weigh up the situation and just how honest he should be; she looked just as lost as her daughter.

"Not the greatest, I'm afraid," he finally replied. "The water alone is near freezing then there are the currents and undertow to contend with - even a strong swimmer would have problems. But," he added quickly, "I have known of worse scenarios that have ended well and we won't stop searching, trust me. Until she's found then I would always say to hold on to hope."

There was silence. Even the puppy had settled down by the side of Axler's foot and was quietly chewing away on his bootlace. Drummond took a sip of tea.

"Mince pie?" asked Mrs Langstone trying to keep control. The plate trembled in her hand.

"Thank you, Mrs Langstone," Drummond took a mince pie. "Now, if it's alright with you, what I'd like is for you to tell me a bit about Holly. I've been to see Sylvia Maddon and now I'd like to hear what you have to say please."

"I'll bet she was horrible about Holly," said Georgie fiercely.

"Why do you say that?" enquired Drummond.

"She's a horrible person herself."

"Georgie," said Mrs Langstone gently and then looked up at Drummond. "Although I have to say Georgie has a point, Inspector Drummond, Sylvia never seemed to like Holly. Mind you, I don't think it was Holly necessarily she didn't like, it was just children, teenagers - well, she never seemed comfortable with them if you see what I mean."

Drummond nodded, having seen Holly's bedroom, he understood exactly what Mrs Langstone was talking about.

"What is Holly like?"

"Well," Mrs Langstone's face softened and she smiled for the first time, "I've known Holly since the day she was born – her mother Sally and I were close friends. Beautiful, beautiful baby, beautiful child. So content and happy. It was an absolute tragedy when Sally died – Holly was only eight when that happened you know - but she and her dad adored each other and they helped each other to carry on. He gave up his job in the City and worked from home so he could be bring her up himself. She was always so happy, definitely very determined and not afraid of anything, she had a lot of friends, the house was always full..."

"... and then Sylvia came along." Georgie spat out the word Sylvia.

"And what happened?" asked Drummond.

"She became very quiet, didn't she dear?" Mrs Langstone turned to Georgie. "It was as if a light had been flicked off. From the outside I could see Sylvia and Holly didn't get on but Holly really tried for her dad's sake to include Sylvia in their life. It didn't work..." she shook her head sadly.

"And then on holiday her dad had that 'accident'" said Georgie mutinously.

Mrs Langstone looked nervous and picked up on Georgie's comment. "He fell from the fourth floor balcony, I'm afraid, there was nothing anyone could do. Again, another tragedy... awful, it was awful..."

"I was on holiday with them when it happened," said Georgie, "and you could tell Sylvia wasn't really upset. Crocodile tears all the time and everybody falls for her act you know, she's so beautiful, they rush around looking after her."

Drummond nodded. "Go on."

"After her dad died Holly just withdrew altogether," chipped in Mrs Langstone. "She put all her energy and concentration into her school work, it was almost as if she was on a mission... She lost so much weight, I was so worried. We both were, weren't we dear?" Georgie nodded vigorously and Mrs Langstone sighed heavily before continuing. "Then Sylvia decided to move to London, away from here – said they both needed a fresh start. I really wanted Holly to stay with us so she could finish school here – her and Georgie were in the same class and have always been best friends – but Sylvia wouldn't hear of it and Holly just quietly said she'd like to go. She kept all her dad's stuff you know..."

An image of neatly stacked brown boxes appeared in Drummond's mind's eye. "Yes, I know," he said gently and then paused a bit. "Can you tell me what happened last night Georgie?"

Georgie's brown eyes welled immediately. "We were having such fun, I'd really missed her and we were just having a great time dancing and talking but then, just before nine thirty I think it was, she said she needed a bit of fresh air and wanted to look at the lights along the bank - we were near Henley I think. It was really cold out so I stayed inside." Her face crumpled. "I should have gone with her, I should have been there..." Fat tears rolled down her cheeks and Mrs Langstone's arms immediately went around her daughter, hugging her tight. The puppy stopped chewing and looked up. Axler bent down and scratched its ears.

Drummond sipped his tea remembering his conversation with Sylvia – she said she hadn't gone looking for Holly until 10.30pm – there was a whole hour when Holly could have been in the water. It really didn't look good.

There was one last question he had to ask and it was the most difficult question of all. He waited until the sobbing had died down. "I'm sorry to ask this Mrs

Langstone, but Mrs Maddon intimated that Holly was depressed, that she may have..."

"She didn't jump!" Georgie jumped to her feet, her round face fierce and hands clenched in anger. "She wouldn't have! She wasn't happy with Sylvia but she really wanted to finish school – she wanted to be an architect like her dad, there's just no way she'd have killed herself. No way!"

Mrs Langstone nodded her head. "I have to agree. Holly really is a very determined young lady. She's seen a lot of tragedy in her young life but she's also had a lot of love and knew she'd find it again - she'd never give up just like that, never."

Drummond considered whether he should ask the next question, it wasn't a good one to ask but before he could Georgie stated. "I think Sylvia had something to do with Holly's disappearance."

"Now why do you think that?" You could have heard a pin drop in the house. Mrs Langstone held her daughter's hand.

Georgie's face fell. "I don't know," she finally admitted. "It's just a feeling – but a strong one! Sylvia never liked Holly that's for sure. She got all the money once Mr Maddon died and she wanted to live well – she always had new designer clothes and stuff. Holly never got a thing you know."

"So why would she want to get rid of Holly?"

There was silence while Georgie chewed her lip in thought. "I don't know, I really don't. But she's not a good person, really, she's not. She's so cold and she was horrible, horrible to Holly. She probably pushed her off just because she was bored of her..."

"Georgie!" Mrs Langstone was shocked.

"No, that's okay Mrs Langstone. It's better out than in," he heard himself saying. "Thank you, thank you for your time, both of you, I think we should go now. It's been a real pleasure to meet you." He stood up, swiftly followed by Axler.

"Now," he patted his pockets searching for his card, "if either of you think of anything, anything at all that could help please call me – day or night. And if I hear anything of Holly I promise I'll call you immediately."

As Mrs Langstone studied the card he could see she was feeling stronger. "Thank you Inspector Drummond," she said. "Thank you for taking the time and trouble to come all the way out here rather than call, we both appreciate it, don't we?" Georgie nodded fiercely. "And if either of us think of anything that might be of help we'll certainly let you know." She took a step towards the door. "Come on twinkle." PC Axler raised his eyebrows and she laughed. "No, not you, sorry. Henry – the puppy," she pointed down at Henry who was still determinedly chewing Axler's shoelaces. She bent down and gently pulled him away. "We're very grateful to you for coming, thank you, Holly's like my second daughter... When you find her, no matter how.. what..." she couldn't find the right words, "please just let us know, won't you?"

Drummond nodded, shook Mrs Langstone's hand and as he left his head was bowed in thought. He wouldn't sleep on the way back to London, he had a lot to do. "Have you still got that laptop in the front Axler?" he asked.

"Yes sir."

"Well, fish it out will you, I've got a bit of work to do."

# UNLUCKY DIP

## SUNDAY, 18 DECEMBER

It was Sunday and Jon woke Holly up just after eleven. He threw open her bedroom door, strode across to the window and drew back the curtains letting crisp winter sunlight flood in.

"Hey, I know how much you need your beauty sleep," he announced loudly, "but we've got to get on with our plans. And," he added, "it's a beautiful day out there – blue sky, birds singing and all that." Groaning, Holly got out of bed and staggered to the bathroom not even glancing in his direction. "Brunch is ready in ten minutes," Jon declared.

"Yeah, I don't eat br..."

"Oh yes you do when you're working with me – need to feed that brain of yours, you've got to be on the ball."

"Brilliant... bloody brilliant... didn't know geeks were so bossy." Holly scratched her head and closed the bathroom door behind her.

Jon grinned and bounced into the kitchen. He'd been up since seven, raring to go but had held back because he knew Holly needed as much sleep as possible. His energy levels were high as he shook the sausages in the frying pan, flipped the bacon, gave the eggs a quick scramble and popped the toast in. He was really looking forward to the day.

Holly appeared exactly ten minutes later, hair still damp.

"Great timing," said Jon. "Carry these." He handed her a full plate of bacon, eggs – the works. She turned pale. "You'll love it when you get started, trust me." Holly grunted.

They sat up at the table this time. Jon, Holly and, of course, Domino who sat up straight in nearby chair closely scrutinising what they were eating. Holly was surprised, once she started eating she found she was actually very hungry and the food quickly disappeared. "All this home cooking is going to make me the size of a whale," she announced as she crunched a piece of crispy bacon. Domino frowned, it wasn't making him fat.

"Is there any more on the news?" she asked as she chewed.

"There's a ton of stuff in the papers and on the net." He pointed to the sofa which was covered in pages of newsprint. "Yours is a very gripping story. But there's not a great deal on the TV now – just that your body still hasn't been found, they're still looking. We'll have to be very careful when we're out, your picture is everywhere."

"Yeah, what it is to be famous..."

The previous evening they'd spent a long time talking and Holly gave as much information as she could to Jon which, frankly, wasn't a great deal when it came down to it; she quickly realised that she knew very little about Sylvia and there still seemed to be no real motive as to why she should want to kill Holly or her father.

"I've run a complete check on Sylvia," said Jon.

Holly put down her fork and swallowed. "A 'complete' check? What does that mean? Are you going to get into trouble?"

"Don't worry, I've been careful, only used safe routes and I've covered my tracks well. The system is quite straightforward and I know my way around."

"System? Do I want to know?"

"Ah well, maybe not... Anyway, there's seriously not a lot to tell – I've got a print out of her previous jobs and, trust me, it's not inspiring reading. Her last job was in Baker, Baker & Sharpe, the Solicitors in Chelmsford you mentioned last night, I'd like to find out more about them but I've only had time to glance through their website – it's pretty archaic. She was in debt at one stage but straightened herself out. Never been married before she met your father and has no previous convictions."

"There's got to be something dodgy in her background," commented Holly.

"You bet," said Jon enthusiastically, "and we're going to find it somewhere in the flat in Kensington. This is going to be great!"

Holly raised her eyebrows. During the course of conversation the previous evening she'd mentioned that most Sunday afternoons, just after lunch, Sylvia went for a walk in Kensington Gardens and then had a coffee in the Starbucks along Ken High Street. As soon as the words had left her lips his eyes had lit up and he'd declared it would be a great opportunity to have a look around the flat.

Holly glanced at her watch, it was already pretty late. "Have we got enough time to get there?"

"Tons, no worries, but you'll have to disguise yourself somehow because we've got to catch a bus into town."

"How are we going to get into the flat? I don't exactly have a key on me."

Jon smiled, his brown eyes enigmatic. "Trust me," he smiled knowingly.

"Trust me," Holly muttered under her breath as she reached up and scratched underneath the tight peroxide wig John had somehow managed to conjure up for her. She'd put on layers of black clothes, a ton of white make-up and her eyes had so much black eyeliner on they looked like tyre marks. Jon had got away with wearing his Iron Maiden t-shirt, black jeans and jacket. They were walking along the richly carpeted corridor towards what had until recently been her home, flat – she wasn't sure what to call it. She glanced across at Jon and got the distinct impression he was loving every minute of this. She scratched underneath her wig again.

"How do you know she's out?" she asked tetchily.

"Trade secret," came the reply.

"Trade secret," mimicked Holly.

"Hey, no making fun of the leader."

"The leader?"

"You want to lead?"

"No, okay, you're the leader. This time."

Jon raised his eyebrows. "Act casual will you?"

"Have you looked in the mirror recently? It's a miracle we've got this far without armed police surrounding us. This is Kensington you know."

Jon pulled a face, getting through the heavy door downstairs caused him no problem whatsoever and he'd quickly whisked them both past the security camera without exposing their faces. "It's not a miracle," he hissed. "It's skill."

Holly grinned but it didn't last, they were outside her front door, number 15.

"Are you ready?" he asked.

She pointed at the door. "How exactly do you know she's not in there and don't give me any of that trade secret stuff."

Jon shrugged. "I just happened to catch sight of her as she turned around the corner going towards Ken High Street." His brown eyes widened and gleamed. "It's all in the timing you know."

"You could have said!"

"What and spoil your fun? Bit of adrenalin is good for you, keeps you on your toes. Hold on…" He tweaked the lock, turned the door handle and pushed the door open. "And here we are."

"How did you do that – you know, like open the door without a key? Is there something you should be telling me?"

"Just something I picked up along the way… You okay?"

Holly took a deep breath and adjusted her wig. "As I'll ever be."

"Come on then. We work quickly – you take the photos. I'll search for the laptop, take a copy of the files and anything else I find."

She waved his mobile. "I'm ready."

The flat was just as sparse and unwelcoming as it had been when she'd left it late Friday afternoon for her party.

"Wow, she certainly goes for minimalism in a big way, doesn't she?" commented Jon drily as he took in the surroundings.

"Oh yeah, just a bit of a neat freak," replied Holly and started snapping. "Her bedroom's down there – first on the left."

Jon disappeared down the hallway.

Holly looked around, there wasn't a great deal to see but she snapped away anyway. She spied a neat pile of paper on the table next to the aluminium tree and walked over. "Don't grab things," Jon had instructed her the previous evening, "look and see first where they're positioned then if you want to move them to get a better look, you know exactly where they belong when you put them back." She surveyed the papers with a professional eye. Lying on top was a business card, she picked it up carefully and read *'Detective Inspector Ian Drummond, Metropolitan Police'*. She put the card back down and took a photograph of it. Then she picked the sheets of paper up one by one and scanned through them. The second sheet down seemed to be the most interesting and she lined it up carefully before taking a picture and then she put everything back in place.

Holly heard a click and a whirl from Sylvia's bedroom and knew that Jon had found Sylvia's laptop and she smiled to herself, he really was good at this kind of stuff, who'd have thought? She walked into the kitchen and opened each cupboard, making a quick search. As usual, there was nothing to eat, all Sylvia had in the flat was coffee and Slimfast, but she took photos as Jon had told her to before walking quietly along the corridor.

She passed Sylvia's room on the left and in a dream made her way to her bedroom, second right along the corridor past the bathroom. She opened the

55

door, turned on the light and made her way along the passageway of boxes to her bed. She picked up the photo lying on the floor and held it to face, feeling its coolness against her skin. "Dad..." she whispered.

"Holly?" she heard a loud whisper.

"In here," she replied and slipped the photo in her pocket.

Jon stood in the doorway and whistled when he saw the boxes lined up. "Wow, she made you live like this?"

"She didn't like clutter," replied Holly sourly. "My memories were apparently clutter, she wanted a fresh start. I kept everything I could..."

Jon walked briskly over and looked down at her, his face serious. "Holly, we'll get your memories and your life back I promise."

"Did you get what you wanted?" she asked quietly.

He stepped back and grinned widely. "And then some," he declared gleefully, waving a memory stick in the air. "Have you got the photos?"

"Yep."

"Everything back where you found it?"

"Exactly oh leader."

He frowned. "I think we've got enough to be going on with and we should leave now. You okay with that?"

A chill crossed over Holly and she shivered. "Oh yes, I'm more than fine with that, come on let's go."

"Being blond really suits you."

"Like shut up will you?"

They closed the door quietly behind them and left the flat. The real work was about to begin.

A black BMW pulled up neatly in the layby opposite the block of flats and the driver, Kevin O'Malley, turned off the engine. Kevin was a young man in his early twenties with cropped blond hair and a face covered with red pimples. He had muscles on muscles. His colleague was called Vincent and came from New York.

Vincent was small and wiry, brown skinned with quick intelligent eyes and was frankly amazed that Kevin had managed to even get behind the steering wheel. "Hey – you going t'be able t'squeeze in there?" he'd asked when they'd first met. Kevin had shrugged, he wasn't big on talking.

"Hey, hey Kev, look at that!" Vincent pointed at Holly and Jon as they emerged from the main door. "Look at that gyrl – youse ever seen hair like that before?"

Kevin grunted. Vincent picked up the camera and took a couple of shots. "Yeah, y'know what? I don't know London much but I'm guessing they don't belong in a posh place like that. Waddya think?"

Kevin shrugged again.

"Yeah I agree," continued Vincent, "but theys only kids I guess – gee if my gyrls ever came home looking like that...."

Jon and Holly disappeared around the corner and Vincent and Kevin continued their surveillance.

The office was open plan. The walls had been painted magnolia some twenty years ago and were now a grubby shade of cappuccino, pockmarked with Blutac stains and covered randomly with duty rota information, calendars, old photos and bits of scribbled on paper. Sickly looking plants drooped, fluorescent lights flickered overhead and the untidy desks were unmanned - with the exception of two of them.

It was 5pm, almost two days since Holly had gone missing.

DI Drummond sighed heavily and switched off his computer, the bright glare of the screen fading quickly. He rubbed his eyes wearily, he'd been collecting information and making phone calls almost the entire day, a thankless task at the best of times but ten times worse on a Sunday when there were few people about. The day was almost over and if he didn't make it home soon his wife would not be happy;

she'd given him quite a lot of leeway because he was trying to find a missing girl but she was flexible only up to a certain point.

He rubbed his chin which, once again, was heavily stubbled and wondered whether he should just give up and grow a beard, but that would probably mean the next stage would creep up on him and he'd end up wearing an anorak, and then he'd have to join a bloody bird watching club or some such thing, his wife would definitely divorce him and he'd end his days on his own...

His train of thoughts were interrupted by an excited "Sir, Sir!!"

PC Axler had come in on his day off and had waded, with impressive concentration and enthusiasm, through piles of information, witness interviews and background checks with Drummond. At this moment in time his boyish face was lit up with a big smile. "Look Sir!" he bounded over to Drummond's table and waved a sheet of paper in front of him. He reminded Drummond of Mrs Langstone's puppy and resisted the urge to grin. "We're not the only ones investigating Sylvia Maddon - another enquiry has been made!"

Drummond snatched the sheet of paper and quickly scanned it. Yes, someone else was making background enquiries about Sylvia. He looked on the other side of the sheet of paper, it was blank. "Who?" he demanded. "Who's been asking?"

"Ah," Axler's face fell. "Sorry Sir, don't know Sir. The enquiry comes from another agency outside the Met." He squinted at the paper then raced back to his computer. "Hold on." Drummond waited while Axler tapped quickly away.

Axler looked up, puzzled, "That's funny Sir, says the enquiry was made by an government agency in France earlier today but there are no more details, it's a classified source. Why d'you think the French would be interested in Sylvia?"

"A French agency?" repeated Drummond thoughtfully.

"'fraid so Sir..."

Drummond's mobile rang shrilly. "Hold on Axler..." he reached over and picked it up. "Sorry love I'm going to be another hour. Yes... I'm sorry, it's to do with the girl... I'll pick up a Chinese on the way home. Tell the kids to behave... well tell him he can't have any Chinese if he doesn't get out of bed... yes, I promise, I won't be long."

He put the phone down and turned to Axler. "I was going to review the information tomorrow morning when I was fresh but suddenly I'm wide awake. You up for going through things, see if we can find a link to our French friends?"

A big grin spread across Axler's face, this was getting interesting. "Yes Sir!"

"Coffee, Axler. We don't have coffee."

"Yes Sir, I'll be 2 minutes..." As he dashed away, sheets of A4 paper swirled off his desk like autumn leaves and floated gently down. Ah, the energy of youth, thought Drummond watching with wry amusement. Where are you, young Holly, he wondered as he bent down to pick up the papers from the worn carpet tiles. Earlier that day as he'd read through her diary he'd noted with surprise that he kept thinking about her and referring to her in the present tense rather than the past. Maybe wishful thinking, he pondered. Her diary was crammed full of her thoughts and hopes and the more he read the more he liked Holly, she'd been through a lot but had dealt with it with courage. However, despite the fact it was obvious she was unhappy, the diary gave no real clues as to whether she felt Sylvia was deliberately targeting her.

Axler came back with two steaming polystyrene cups of coffee. Drummond took one and sniffed it suspiciously – he always did and with good reason, God only knew what was in the damn stuff the machine served up, he doubted it had ever seen a real coffee bean.

"Thanks," he muttered and blew on the surface to cool it. "Right, come on then Axler, let's see what you've learnt." He walked over to a large whiteboard, produced a fat black marker pen from his jacket pocket and looked at the blank surface.

"What do we know so far about young Holly?" he asked. Axler was standing quite close behind him, arms folded, face serious. Drummond had been surprised by Axler's attitude who he'd presumed was just another beat bobby, but here he was on his day off helping with the boring leg work – in his experience most officers would have gone off sick rather than be faced with a pile of forms and leads to follow. Information gathering, putting in requests for basic information from various government agencies and dealing with red tape was not a lot of fun.

"She doesn't have any living relatives that I can find - no grandparents, no aunts, no nothing Sir. Mrs Langstone and her daughter Georgie appear the people closest to her. When her father died Holly didn't seem to inherit anything but we've yet to see a copy of his Will."

Drummond was drawing his version of a mind map on the whiteboard. He'd written the name Holly, circled it then drew a few lines outwards making it look like a fat spider. Called Holly.

"Now, Axler - Sylvia..." He wrote the name Sylvia in capital letters at the end of one of the spider's legs.

Axler's face lit up, they'd discovered a number of interesting facts about Sylvia. "Thirty two years old. Maiden name Smith, Sir. No past record to speak of. Did a few secretarial and receptionist jobs in London, even did a bit of modelling, but she never got into any trouble although at one point she ran up a few credit cards and got into debt, but nothing too major." Drummond's pen squeaked as he wrote down the information on the whiteboard. The fluorescent light flickered overhead and he frowned in concentration.

"Now this is the interesting bit Sir. About an hour ago I spoke to Mr Robert Baker the Senior Partner at Baker, Baker & Sharpe the solicitors in Chelmsford where Sylvia worked. Sylvia started work there almost exactly two years ago on recommendation from someone but he can't remember who.

"It turns out that Mr Maddon was one of Mr Sharpe's clients and he seems to remember that Sylvia first met Maddon when he visited the office on business. It was, it would appear, love at first sight and they got married just under a year ago. Mr Maddon died in an accident on holiday in Barbados this August as Mrs Langstone said." Axler flicked through some papers. "There was an enquiry as a matter of formality because it was an unexpected death and the verdict was recorded as accidental death."

"Hmm…" mused Drummond out loud as he wrote quickly trying to catch up. "Love, marriage, death – all in under two years, bit of a rollercoaster…"

He turned to Axler. "She continued working at the Solicitors after they were married?"

"Yes Sir."

"But left there soon after Mr Maddon's death?"

"Yes Sir."

Squeak squeak squeak went the marker pen.

Drummond turned to face Axler. "She's not working at the moment is she? She's not on benefits either so how do you suppose she's supporting herself? How did she manage to buy that flat in Kensington? Probably used the money from Maddon's estate but I should imagine it must be almost gone by now – he wasn't a hugely wealthy man by all accounts. How is she planning to live? Did Maddon take out a life insurance policy? Axler?"

"Not that I've discovered Sir. Maybe she's thinking of getting a job in London but on a receptionist's money is that enough to run a flat and support a teenager?"

"No, no, I don't think it is Axler. Teenagers inhale money, trust me... Now, what if she's living like this because she knows – expects – something else is going to happen, something that will rescue her?"

A big smile spread across Axler's face and he rocked back on his heels. "Sounds reasonable Sir."

"And..." Drummond hesitated, waving the marker pen like a wand in front of him, "the one thing that keeps bugging me is the fact that she was concerned with how long it would take before Holly could be declared dead. Now, if the girl has no money, why would that be of interest to her? Eh? What do you think?"

"That there's a very strong possibility that money's involved somewhere along the line Sir. As Holly's legal guardian she would inherit anything Holly owned – that would solve the problem of how she supports herself. We just need a copy of Mr Maddon's Will. Robert Baker assured me we'd have a copy by first thing tomorrow morning – he said he'd see if he could scan it tonight and e-mail it over but couldn't promise that because it's Sunday and he's no good "at doing this scanning lark" without his secretary's help.

Drummond nodded, good... and wrote the word 'money' linking it with Holly's name and also Sylvia's.

"Now Axler, this name Sharpe that keeps cropping up..."

Axler screwed up his face in thought and opened his mouth to speak.

"Hold on a minute," said Drummond and wrote SHARPE in capital letters at the end of another spider leg and drew a circle around it.

"You'll need two of those, Sir," said Axler. "There are two Sharpes."

"Really? Go on then Axler, tell me about them."

"David Sharpe, of course, is a partner at Baker, Baker & Sharpe," said Axler. "He's almost near retirement. Never been in trouble as far as we're aware. Wife is a teacher at a local school."

"And Sharpe Enterprises? Is this the same Sharpe? Or another one?" Drummond hadn't forgotten the name on the letter headed paper.

"Sharpe Enterprises is a small agency specialising in purchasing and selling land on behalf of large organisations and rich people who need to invest money, Sir. Can't see a connection with the solicitors but I'm betting there is one. It's also based in Chelmsford. It's owned by a *Mark* Sharpe – no one else involved. We have no other information on him although I've put in a request for more detailed background search."

"Maybe they're relatives?" Drummond's marker pen firmly marked a black dot underneath a question mark.

"Could be Sir."

"Axler, tomorrow we'll concentrate on finding out more about Sharpe Enterprises, I've got a gut feeling about it – whatever's going on we're going to get to the bottom of it. First thing in the morning we'll drive down to Chelmsford to pick up the Will if need be and find out more about this Mark Sharpe and what exactly his company does."

"Ah… Sir, sorry Sir, I'm back on duty tomorrow." Axler's young face was full of disappointment. "But I can come in when my shift finishes at two, I'd like to continue be involved." He smiled hopefully and uncertainly.

Drummond frowned in thought; damn, he'd got carried away and had completely forgotten Axler was doing this in his own time. Tomorrow morning he'd have to see the Chief Super, go over things with him and convince him to give him Axler as a resource.

"Leave that to me Axler. Go on duty as usual and wait for a call."

"Sir." Axler tried not to look too pleased.

"Now then Axler. There's got to be a link between Sharpe Enterprises, the Solicitors, Maddon and Sylvia. Enough for two possible murders. And," he paused, "enough to make the French interested... Any link that you can see?"

Axler sipped his coffee and looked at the middle aged, intense, unshaven and untidy man in front of him. He was starting to like him. "Nope, can't see a link, Sir but I have no doubt that we'll find one."

"Hmm," Drummond considered. "I have a feeling we will Axler. Now," he threw the empty polystyrene cup in the bin, "I've just got one more call to make and then I'd better get home or my wife will have me. I'll speak to you tomorrow."

Sylvia lay on her bed fully clothed staring up at the white ceiling. She wouldn't lie on her side in case her make up rubbed off on the pillow slip. Tears pricked her eyes but she wouldn't cry, what if the mascara ran and someone came to the door and then what would they think? Her seamless face creased for a moment, who was she kidding? No one would come and knock on her door, she'd isolated herself from everyone. People loved to look at her because she was beautiful, she knew that, but she was like the ice maiden, untouchable. She knew no one in London but then she didn't want to know anyone other than Mark.

A soft sigh escaped her lips. She was so tired and so alone but when Mark had called earlier that evening he'd said it would be some time, maybe even a week now, before they could see each other again because of all the police and press interest. He said she may even have to start looking for a job. A job! For goodness sakes he'd promised she'd never had to work again! Hot tears pricked her eyes again. She was the one who'd had to make all the sacrifices, not him. She was the one who'd had to endure two years in a backwater solicitors office with the most boring people on earth and then marry a man she didn't love and share the house with an annoying brat of a teenager who did nothing but moon about gazing after her father like she'd lost something. She was the one who had to charm the authorities, the police, coroners and everyone. She was the one who had killed two people. She'd fulfilled her end of the bargain over and over again. She'd worked so hard. It wasn't fair! And then for him to back off and leave her to cope on her own... He'd said she'd been impulsive, rash - what happens he'd said, if they can't find the body and it takes months before she can be declared dead? The deadline is coming up and if we miss it all that money will disappear.

Her blue eyes iced over as she remembered his words. That money was not going to someone else, not after everything she'd had to endure.

Sylvia sat up abruptly and stretched before walking through to the kitchen. She smiled as she entered, she loved its cool clean lines and simplicity - like a showroom kitchen she thought. Her feet though, were bare and the tiled floor was cold and she sighed again. She opened the fridge. Nothing in there, not even a pint of milk. She opened a cupboard, damn, only one can of Slimfast looked back at her and she slammed the door shut. God, where was chocolate when you needed it? Maybe she should go and get something, it was Sunday evening but the corner shop would be open, it always was. Mind you, the smell of cheap groceries always made her feel sick when she went in there. One day, she thought, one day I'll order my food from Harrods and I'll never have to go into a damn supermarket again.

Her mobile rang and she jumped. Mark, it had to be, she could feel it. Oh my God what if he started ranting again? He'd been so horrible to her... Maybe he was calling to apologise? She took a big breath and picked up the phone. "Mrs Maddon?" A deep masculine voice asked.

"Yes?"

"Detective Inspector Drummond here."

Oh yes, the grubby policeman with the ugly face who'd come to see her yesterday afternoon.

"Oh hello again Inspector Drummond," she replied sweetly. Then she looked at the clock on the wall, why would he be calling her now? News, it had to be! Oh my God, they'd found her! Holly was dead, everything would be alright, she'd be rich and marry Mark!

"Mrs Maddon?"

"Sorry, sorry," she replied trying to even her tone. "Have you found Holly?"

"No, I'm afraid not. I'm sorry if I got your hopes up. Really, I was just calling to let you know we're all still working hard and that we'll keep you regularly posted. We're looking at all aspects."

"All aspects?" She twiddled her hair nervously.

"We're working closely with the London Coastguard and they're still searching the obvious places – and the not so obvious places as well I should say."

"Oh."

"Are you alright Mrs Maddon? Are you holding up okay?"

What did he want, an invitation to come around?

"Yes, yes, I'm fine thanks, coping, you know. I'll be pleased though when they find her so she can finally have some peace." She tapped her front teeth nervously, a habit Mark hated and that she was trying to stop. She wanted to ask about the diary but didn't dare.

"Yes, I understand. Well, Mrs Maddon, I'm off duty now but other officers are working on this but I'll call you immediately should anything come to light."

"Thank you Inspector Drummond. Goodnight. And thank you for your help." God damn where was the girl? She slammed her hands down on the kitchen table and resisted the urge to scream. Just how hard could it be to find a body?

Her mobile rang again and she jumped.

"Sylvia?"

"Yes Mark?"

"Who was that on the phone – it went into the answering service so I know you were talking to someone."

Why was he always so suspicious of her?

"The police, the Drummond guy who came around yesterday. And no they haven't found her. And yes I am aware of the deadline. And no, I haven't made any more *mistakes*." She walked into the living room as she spoke to him, edgy and restless. She moved the pile of correspondence on the dining room table over an inch and then back again into its original spot – I'd better shred that or he'll accuse me of being careless again she thought.

"Are you still upset?" asked a honeyed voice.

She paused and then nodded determinedly. "Yes Mark, yes, I am upset. I've worked incredibly hard and now the damn girl may never be found and you think it's all my fault. Well, you tell me how you would have got rid of her." She held the phone to her ear and frowned as she gazed out of the window at people walking in the street below, a group of them were on their way to a Christmas party already tanked up, shouting and laughing, waving bottles of cheap wine.

"Well, you have to admit it could have been better thought out darling." Hmm, 'darling' he'd obviously calmed down. But still no apology she noted, hanging her head in thought.

"Sylvia?"

"Yes?"

"Goodnight. I promise we'll meet as soon as possible."

"Okay," she replied vacantly and closed the phone shut. She walked away from the window and picked up the remote, turning the television on but didn't sit down and watch it, it was just good to have a noise in the background. She picked up the pile of correspondence from the table and sorted through it putting aside the letter from Sharpe Enterprises to shred. That took less than one minute. She looked up and around then walked out of the living room and into her bedroom. She opened a cupboard and scrabbled about, pulled on a pair of brown ankle boots and her red jacket; she'd go to the corner shop and buy a bottle of wine. Maybe two. And a freakin party hat.

As she walked along the corridor she passed by Holly's bedroom. She hesitated for a moment then stopped, turned and slowly opened the door. Turned off, Holly's stupid fairy lights looked like heavy black cobwebs draped along the cardboard boxes. Damn it! Damn Holly and her damn boxes and her damn memories and her damn diary.

Her stomach growled and she hesitated, maybe Holly had hidden some chocolate, she was always whingeing about being hungry. She strode down the narrow walk way to Holly's bed and threw back the duvet, then she hurled the pillow to the other side of the room. It knocked over the stupid Christmas tree on the desk. Nothing. She fell to her knees and hunted under the bed. Nothing. She started to laugh. Stupid, stupid, she was stupid. Pull yourself together Sylvia she whispered to herself as she stood up.

She dusted herself down and looked around at the room. Soon, she thought, soon all this rubbish would be gone – recycled, whatever. Gone. Then she turned on her heel and walked out of the flat, slamming the door behind her.

As she left the building and strode down the street Vincent hopped quickly out of the car glad of the opportunity to stretch his legs and get some fresh air and followed at a discreet distance.

Holly and Jon's journey home from Sylvia's flat had been made in silence, both of them lost in thought. The first thing Jon had done when they arrived back at the flat was to turn on the laptop and download the information from the memory stick.

The first thing Holly did was to tear off the wig, scratch her scalp long and hard and then take a hot shower to get rid of the thick white make up. By the time she emerged, fresh and clean Jon was already lost, engrossed, typing a hundred words a minute it seemed and pausing only occasionally to look into space for a second or two in thought. After an hour though, he seemed disappointed and drummed his fingers impatiently on the keyboard. "It's just the usual rubbish people keep on their computers but even less somehow – she doesn't seem to have any friends or family that she writes to, no messenger files, e-mails, nothing...

"Probably doesn't have friends or family – my theory is that she isn't actually human." Holly had pulled up a chair next to him and was watching him work. "I think she was hatched."

Jon raised his eyebrows. "Evil fledgling or not, there is just one person whose name seems to pop up occasionally in her documents - Mark Sharpe. Do you know him? And where did you put the mobile? I'll download the photos."

"Sorry, I was in such a rush to get changed, it's still in my pocket... hold on..." Holly handed the mobile over and Mark started downloading. "The solicitor's office Sylvia worked for in Chelmsford was called Baker, Baker & Sharpe. I met Mr Sharpe once when we had to pick her up for lunch, I don't remember his first name but he was like middle aged - seemed okay," she said.

"Hmm," Jon's fingers immediately started tapping. "I seem to remember I looked the firm up yesterday – let's see what happens when I do a search on just the name Sharpe... here we go... ah," Jon was disappointed. "His name is David Sharpe, not Mark and he's one of the Partners and yes, you're right," he studied the picture on the front page of the website, "he seems pretty average."

"Mind you, dad always told me to be careful of the quiet ones," commented Holly.

"Hold on, there's another Sharpe here in Chelmsford – yes, Mark – it's got to be the same one she's been writing to. There's got to be some kind of connection between the two Sharpes and Sylvia." Mark looked at Holly.

"I found a letter from a company called Sharpe something on the table," said Holly. "It's one of the first photos I took – pull it up, maybe we can find a clue there?"

Jon urgently tapped the keyboard. Drummond's business card appeared on screen.

"Next one."

The letter flipped up and they both leaned forward to read it.

"My oh my," said Jon admiringly. "I think we've got it."

Holly's eyes widened as she read. The letter, addressed to Sylvia, was confirmation that Sharpe Enterprises was interested in buying a plot of land she was in possession of just to the north of Chelmsford on behalf of an American company called Ladyluck Corporation.

"Land?" she whispered. "What land? I didn't know she had any land and she hates Chelmsford."

Jon's eyes were sparking with energy. "This is the key Holly, there's a ton of information here I can follow up on – you …." The shrill tone of the telephone interrupted him and distracted, he picked it up. "Oh hi Dad. How are you? Yes, I'll get the girls and the drink out of the house before you come home…" He raised his eyebrows. "… Only joking dad, nah, I'm okay honest. Doing my coursework – yes, of course…" Holly noticed he closed his eyes when he lied, good job his dad couldn't see him or he wouldn't stand a chance.

"Yep, I've still got enough money, no problem. How are things there?" He listened carefully for a few moments. "Well, just keep thinking of the Christmas bonus... Yes, I'm fine, really you don't have to worry. I've met up with Matt and James and Emma – she dragged us all around the shops, you know what she's like..." He listened intently for a moment. "Yes, Dom's fine, eating everything in sight. No, don't worry I'll make sure the place is clean when you get back. Yes, see you in a few days, love you dad... yep, bye..."

He flushed and pushed his hair back. "My dad..." he said.

Holly smiled. "You were so sweet," she teased. "You really love your dad don't you?"

Jon shrugged his slim shoulders. "Dad practically brought up Alex and me on his own when mum left. Yeah, he has a go at me because I'm on the computer all the time, but he'd do anything for me." He caught sight of Holly's face and was immediately contrite. "Oh I'm so sorry Holly, I didn't mean to say that when your dad is..."

Holly stood firm. "No, Jon, it's okay - you can't watch everything you say in case you hurt my feelings really you can't. I just want to sort this all out, afterwards I'll have a good cry."

There was a long silence. "You know," said Jon, "I have a feeling that we're in for the long haul." He strode out to the kitchen. "Coffee, I need coffee and cake. You coming?"

"Don't drink coffee but I'll have a coke and cake," she replied and turned to stare hard at the screen. Land, Ladyluck Corporation – her stomach churned. She knew instinctively that Jon was right, they'd hit the jackpot, and that the answers were close. "How can I help?" She followed Jon into the kitchen. "I can't just sit here and watch you do all the work."

Jon was stirring milk into the mug. "Look, when I work it's pretty intense, I get really geared into what I'm doing – it's a geek thing. What I'll do is print everything out, you can read it and collate all the information - put it all together so we can go through it all afterwards. I've got a feeling it's going to be a long evening."

She nodded and they both settled down to work. Jon did indeed work intensely, following one lead after another on the computer, sending page after page of information to print. Holly cleared a large area on the living room floor and started the long process of reading and sorting.

It was past 10 o'clock when Jon finally broke away from the computer. "Argh!" he cried, dramatically rubbing his eyes. "They burn, they burn! Hey, hold on, can you hear something?"

Holly listened carefully. A faint but persistent meow filtered through from the corridor outside.

"Oh no, it's Dom, I'd forgotten all about him and he's been out all day. I'll bet that's one unhappy cat," said Jon. "He always is when he's hungry – if I were you I wouldn't get in his way, he might eat you." He strode over and opened the front door and Domino stalked in jerking his tail. Jon bent to scratch his head but Dom neatly ducked and headed straight for the kitchen.

"Oops," said Jon. "I'd better feed him, it's about time we had a break anyway. You want a sandwich or something?"

Holly nodded, the evening had sped by but she was starving now. She stood in the doorway, arms crossed and watched him as he sped efficiently around the kitchen. "You were right," she grinned, "you really are a computer genius aren't you? It's brilliant all the stuff you've found."

Jon hunkered down and spooned food into Dom's bowl. "Hmm, I've never used it quite like this before, my teacher would have a fit if he could see what I'm doing – probably wouldn't know whether to give me extra credit or report me to the police..."

Holly laughed. "What about your dad?"

"Well with a bit of luck he may never find out about all this but I'll just play that by ear." He straightened up. "Now, that sandwich..."

"Can I do anything?"

"Nope, it's okay, I kinda like doing this, helps me concentrate somehow..."

Holly stood up straight. "There's something I need to talk to you about."

"Yes?" He expertly sliced a tomato.

"Georgie..."

Jon was buttering some bread but turned to look at her.

"Look, I know what you're going to say," said Holly. "Really I do. I just want to speak to her so badly, she's my best friend in the world and she must be sick with worry about me..."

Jon opened his mouth.

"However," Holly put up a hand and continued. "I know I can't get in touch with her can I? Not until we know exactly what we're up against and have proof. If I'm right and Sylvia did kill dad as well as try to kill me then Georgie could be put into danger if she knows anything. Right?"

"Right," said Jon. "Only the two of us know you're alive and that's the way it's got to be for the time being."

"Oh my God," groaned Holly banging the doorframe with her head. "If Sylvia doesn't get me first Georgie is just so going to kill me! We've told each other everything since we started school, we've never had any secrets..."

Jon handed Holly her sandwich. "You'll be able to tell her soon. I'm pretty sure some of this stuff I'm pulling up from the web is starting to make sense - we're unearthing an awesome can of worms."

Holly had to admit she'd felt a growing excitement throughout the evening as she'd read through the mass of accumulated information. "Come on then," she directed. "Let's go finish detecting on the sofa."

# UNLUCKY DIP

They sat on the settee side by side with papers scattered all over the coffee table in front of them and munched hungrily on their sandwiches. Jon went quickly over the information they'd put together. "Right," he said through mouthfuls of sandwich, "I'll tell you how I understand it so far and you fill in any gaps. Okay?"

"Okay."

"First point - the land referred to in the letter that we *think* belongs to Sylvia is just north of Chelmsford. Ladyluck Corporation is interested in buying it."

"Yep."

"Second point - Ladyluck Corporation is an American Company that is run with a rod of iron by its President Max Henderson. Ladyluck is huge, its turnover is more than some of the smaller countries of the world. According to the newspapers, three years ago Max Henderson spent over a million pounds buying a large parcel of land north of Chelmsford. The UK company that negotiated the buying of this land on their behalf is Sharpe Enterprises run by Mark Sharpe. Coincidence?"

"I don't think so," commented Holly drily.

"Ladyluck plan to build the first ever Las Vegas style Casino in the UK on that plot of land."

"It was on the news some time ago, I remember dad was interested – I'm sure there were other companies putting in bids though weren't there?"

Jon waved a sheaf of papers. "Oh yes, but this particular tender looks *very* promising – the site is close to London, Stansted, major routes going north and south. It would be ideal and it's the main contender apparently."

"So," commented Holly, "there are two bits of land, both north of Chelmsford. Ladyluck Corporation has bought one and is interested in buying the other. Sharpe Enterprises is involved in both negotiation deals. Yes?"

"Yep. We really need to access the council's planning information and pinpoint these two pieces of land. Third main point," Jon chewed thoughtfully and then swallowed the last of his sandwich. "These local newspapers really are a fund of information... Mark Sharpe is David Sharpe's son, there was an article about them at a charity function – pillars of the local community apparently. I reckon Baker, Baker & Sharpe are somehow involved in this land stuff."

"The solicitors where Sylvia worked and..." Holly muttered. "Oh my goodness, and... that my dad used to use before he even met her..."

"Yes!" Jon punched the air and leapt to his feet scattering papers all over the floor. He paced up and down. Domino glowered at him.

"Your dad actually used Baker, Baker & Sharpe for legal stuff?"

"Yes, God, I hadn't really thought about it before now – I just always thought of it as the place where Sylvia worked."

Jon's brain was working things out quickly. "That's the icing on the cake. There's such an incredible link here Holly, it's like a web – Sylvia, your father, Mark Sharpe, the solicitors, Ladyluck Corporation – they really are all connected." He waved his arms about as he paced up and down. "This piece of land must have something to do with Sylvia's attempt to murder you – just think about it, if you or your father own land that's connected somehow to this multi-million pound casino deal you could name your own price – you'd be rich beyond your dreams. Did your father ever mention anything about land?"

Holly shrugged her shoulders. "No nothing. No land was ever mentioned – ever."

Jon cracked his knuckles. "Ok, then I need to access some records and find out once and for all who owns it."

"You can do that?"

UNLUCKY DIP

"Oh yeah, you just watch me." His fingers flew over the keyboard, hunger forgotten.

Holly got up from the sofa and walked over to him and put her hand on his shoulder. He stopped typing and looked up, her face was expressionless and he felt uneasy.

"We are going to get her aren't we?" she asked.

"Yes, I really think we are. Look, we have to be sensible about this – we don't know anything yet for certain, we've got to double check every bit of information we find. I know I got a bit excited then but we may not be right, we might be going down the wrong road." He paused for a moment and rolled his eyes. "Oh my God, I sounded just like my father then..." he shook his head sadly.

"But it makes sense doesn't it?" Holly shook his arm to get him to pay attention. "My dad has some land that Sharpe Enterprises needs but instead of going to him this Mark person and Sylvia work together. They killed my dad. But why me? She inherited everything anyway."

"Unless the land wasn't your father's – it was yours, even though you didn't know about it," suggested Jon quietly.

"Oh my God." Holly sat down heavily on the floor her head buried in her hands. "That's what happened, isn't it? She killed my dad and tried to kill me so she could inherit a stupid bit of land. I'd have given it to her if she'd asked, if it would have saved my dad... Do you think she's planned this for years, that she deliberately made dad love her and then killed him?"

Jon didn't know how to reply. Silence filled the room for long minutes and when Holly finally looked up her face was calm, her grey eyes as hard as flint, her voice cold. "We need to find out everything. I'm going to make sure she's locked up for good unless I get to her first in which case I won't be responsible for my actions. Or what about this Max Henderson, head of Ladyluck, I'm sure I read somewhere that he's

76

involved in mob stuff – maybe we could contact him and arrange to take her out? I'll give him the land for free."

"Er... well, for one thing we don't know that he isn't mixed up in it already," replied Jon uneasily. "And I don't think taking her out like that will solve anything although maybe..." He paused for a moment as he considered whether it would solve anything. "No, no Holly, let's just find out as many facts as we can first then we can deal with mobsters and stuff okay? Look, we can go to this Inspector Drummond you know, you've read what I've pulled up on him, he seems a decent guy. Holly are you listening to me?"

Holly staring into mid distance. "Yes, I hear you Jon and yes I know you're right but if the opportunity comes along I'd like to take her out myself, okay?"

"You got it," he said finally and continued his search.

# UNLUCKY DIP

**MONDAY, 19 DECEMBER:**
**1am London time / 5pm (Sunday) Las Vegas**

The man was an African American in his mid-fifties, clean shaven with chiselled, handsome features and close cropped white hair. His shoulders were broad, his stomach flat and his body muscular and lean due to the discipline of harsh exercise every day. The sharp and stylish suit he wore cost more than an average person's monthly wage but it was his presence that made people sit up when he walked into a room. He was a predator, smart, intelligent and extremely dangerous. No one crossed him. This was Max Henderson, President of Ladyluck Corporation.

Max had been born and brought up on the violent backstreets of Las Vegas. His mother was a mediocre showgirl in a city that did not tolerate mediocrity and by the age of 24 she was waitressing in diners to get by. He'd never known who his father was but Max needed no one to guide him, he knew exactly what he wanted - power and everything that brought with it, and in Las Vegas that meant one thing, controlling the gambling industry. Max set about achieving his aim in a clinical, logical manner.

When he was 16 he joined the Army specifically to learn discipline and leadership skills, how to orchestrate and manage a war and, of course, how to kill effectively. In down time, while his friends were out enjoying themselves he studied Business Management and achieved a double first. He worked hard and did supremely well in all aspects, and when he returned 7 years later to the streets of Las Vegas he was more than prepared. A new style of leadership had arrived in town - organised and systematic. Many of the men he employed he knew from his army days and he trained and organised them along military lines expecting complete obedience and discipline. Despite his youth he quickly became a force to be reckoned with and the local gangsters realised that Max and his newly formed and tightly run company were not to be trifled with.

He developed his own strict code of honour. First and foremost he was a patriot. He was absolutely loyal to the United States of America and those he employed were expected to be loyal to their country and himself without question; he recognised and handsomely rewarded loyalty in those who worked for him and simply disposed of those who failed to meet the mark.

The world of gambling was a war ground in itself because the stakes – money and power - were supremely high and Max prided himself that those who opposed him were dealt with swiftly, believing that a quick death sent the exactly same message as a slow death. Many died during the first years of his return to Las Vegas.

Both the local police force and FBI had a healthy respect for Max Henderson because once he'd established himself as the number one person in charge there was stability and orderliness to his criminal empire. They could never pin anything on him but their files on him would have filled several of his casinos.

He was, of course, wealthy in the extreme but never indulged in unnecessary luxury as his several ex-wives would testify with bitterness. He saw himself as something of a frontiersman and was always on the lookout for new challenges and opportunities. Just over three years ago the British government, always on the look-out for extra cash, had decided to establish its own small city dedicated to gambling – a mini Las Vegas, and Max Henderson knew without any shadow of doubt that he would be the one to set it up. The bid was thrown open to anyone who was interested and the race was on – from all corners of the world, those involved in the gambling world put their best men on the case and started to design the ultimate Casino City. The British government rubbed their hands as they watched the scramble and dreamt of all the millions they would make in tax. Max never once wavered in his belief and determination that he would win the bid. His jaw tightened as he stared out of a window of his penthouse suite at the bright lights of the city below him. It was just after 5pm on a Sunday evening. Sunday, a day that should mean peace and quiet, but this was Las Vegas and his mind, like the rest of the city, was razor sharp.

"Tell me exactly what happened Schultz." He always called his employees by their surname, never once giving them a chance to become familiar with him.

Schultz shifted his feet, he was a big beefy man, his suits were always a size too small and his hair was so closely cropped he seemed almost bald. Despite the cool air conditioning his face was red and blotchy and his palms were sweaty from stress. Even though he'd worked for Henderson for thirty years he'd never felt comfortable in his company. I could just so do without this, he thought, I'm so close to retirement and that beach house in Miami with Gina...

"Ladyluck Corporation," Schultz stood to attention and spoke to Henderson's back, "commissioned a company in the UK – Sharpe Enterprises - to buy land for the casino bid. It's owned and run by a Mr Mark Sharpe. We identified the company as being small and easily controlled, like the ones we often use over here. Sharpe bought the land on our behalf three years ago." He paused and resisted the urge to wipe the sweat from his forehead. He knew that Henderson, even with his back to him, would notice and consider it a weakness.

"We discovered the other day, however, that Mark Sharpe provided false information and altered documentation. He lied. Although he bought the land that Casino City will be built on, it seems he didn't buy the land that gives access to it. Without the access land, of course, we will have no city at all. Our legal department didn't pick up the error Sir."

Henderson turned swiftly on his heel and marched up to Schultz until his face was just a couple of inches away from Schultz's and his black eyes looked enquiringly into Schultz's blue eyes. What terrified Schultz was that you could never tell when Henderson was angry – heck, half the time you couldn't tell if he was alive he was so composed.

"Who exactly owns the access land?" asked Henderson politely.

"It's complicated, Sir - a girl, Holly Maddon – but it depends on whether she's dead or not." Shaking slightly, Schultz opened a beige file he'd been clutching. "Holly Maddon," he read. "15 years old now. The land was left to her years ago by her Godfather."

"Sharpe. Tell me about Sharpe." Henderson hadn't moved, he was still two inches away from Shultz.

Schultz couldn't stop himself, he raised a hand and wiped his face. "It seems that not buying the land was initially an oversight on his part but, once he realised his mistake - some two years ago now - rather than come clean to us, he set up a complicated plot so that he could get his hands on the land himself."

"It would appear he knows nothing about how I conduct business doesn't it Schultz?"

Schultz managed a small smile. "Sharpe arranged for his girlfriend Sylvia to meet Mr Maddon, Holly's father, who was a widower and they got married just over a year ago. This summer Mr Maddon had an 'accident' when they were on holiday in Barbados – he fell from a hotel balcony and died - there was a brief enquiry and it was put down as accidental death.

"Last Friday evening, Holly's birthday, it seems that she also met with an accident – Sylvia is making out that Holly threw herself over the side of a riverboat on the Thames out of grief for her father. No body has been found and Sylvia will, in theory, inherit the land on confirmation of Holly's death. I presume the plan is that she and Mark Sharpe sell the land to us for an inflated sum and share the money."

Schultz watched, hypnotised as a muscle twitched and pulsed on the side of Henderson's neck. He fully expected to be shot. His body would never be found, probably left somewhere out in the desert for wild dogs. Gina would move to Miami, get the little beach house they'd dreamed of together and marry someone else. Depression swamped him.

"Get rid of Sharpe," came the curt command. "He's vermin and he's compromised the deal. We don't need him. We'll find another way." He finally moved away from Schultz and walked over to his desk.

Schultz swallowed, it had been a few years since he'd had orders to take someone out. Still, he considered, it would be like the old days and he needed a break and maybe London would be good this time of year – Christmas never felt like Christmas in Las Vegas, all this damn heat. Not like his home town of New York where you wrapped up warm and sometimes it snowed...

"Holly Maddon." Henderson interrupted this thoughts and touched a school photograph of Holly that had fallen out of the file onto his desk, an identical copy of the one that Drummond had been given by Sylvia. "I don't like unnecessary death especially in one so young. You say her body has not been found?"

"No Sir."

"The cops. What are they doing?"

"It seems the British police are not dumb, they're suspicious of Sylvia and are making background enquiries. The guy in charge is called Drummond, an old fashioned cop with good instincts. He already knows about the land, Sharpe Enterprises and the fact they were acting on our behalf when they bought it but that is, of course, public knowledge anyway. He'll soon have a copy of Maddon's Will, if he hasn't already got it, which will prove that Holly inherited the access land. We have someone on the inside keeping an eye on what's happening. Sharpe and Sylvia Maddon don't have a clue the police are interested in them."

"And what else Schultz?"

Schultz sometimes wondered if Max had a third eye. "There's another party involved Sir. They've been making background enquiries about Sylvia Maddon – we picked this up from our guy on the inside."

"Who is it?"

"We're working on it Sir."

"Work harder Schultz."

Henderson sat down in his black leather chair then leaned forward and flexed his fingers, knuckles cracking. His eyes were like steel as he read each sheet of paper from the file and carefully studied and memorised each bit of information. Schultz stood in front of the desk and waited. He didn't say anything. He knew better. Henderson had a mind that was quick, analytical and ruthless and he didn't like being interrupted.

"Schultz. You are to go to London now and oversee this. Get rid of Mark Sharpe and don't leave a trail. Sylvia Maddon..." He picked up a photo of her, she was stunning but her beauty was meaningless - beauty came from within, from honour. She had married a man merely to kill him and his daughter. He looked at the photograph of Drummond and allowed himself a glimmer of a smile at the irony - the man had a face that looked like a road accident but had an honourable soul. Schultz noted the lip twitch but didn't know what it meant.

"Scare her but don't kill her at the moment, it would be too suspicious."

"Yes Sir, we already have her under surveillance – Vincent Merino, the best," replied Schultz.

Henderson didn't look up. "Keep her controlled, she's a killer but she's an amateur. Use your discretion, however, and if she becomes a problem get rid of her. Holly, we need to find out as soon as possible what's happened to her and if she's alive I want her, do you understand? I'll be in London in a couple of days' time."

"Yes Sir."

"I still intend to put in that bid and to win," continued Henderson. "There'll be a way of obtaining this land. Control this situation until I get there myself. Time is of the essence and Schultz?"

"Sir?"

"Make no mistakes."

"I won't Sir. The jet's ready to leave in half an hour for London. I'll control the operation there; I *will* get that land for you Mr Henderson."

"I expect nothing less from you," replied Henderson drily. "Now go. On your way out tell my Assistant to get the Head of Legal here now."

Schultz practically ran out of the room. His suit was wringing wet and seemed to have shrunk another size but Hell, he was alive. Henderson watched Schultz leave, he knew he'd do the task well, they'd worked together for many years and he trusted him. He also knew Schultz would not want to mess up his retirement plans in Miami with Gina – keep them motivated, give them a purpose to do well, he thought.

He got up and walked over the window again, watching Las Vegas as it stretched and woke up for another busy evening. He allowed himself a glimmer of a smile for the second time that day. He liked a challenge.

It had just gone one o'clock in the morning when the flickering fluorescent light finally died with a sad pop. Axler looked up and sighed with relief, it had been driving him crazy for hours.

# UNLUCKY DIP

When Drummond had left the officer earlier that evening, curiosity had got the better part of Axler and he'd stayed on tapping quietly away on his computer, trawling through internet sites. Although he'd come to a dead end investigating the French agency that had requested a search on Sylvia, he'd been able to gather a lot of information about Mark Sharpe which had then led him to a search on Ladyluck Corporation. And, although he didn't have a copy of the letter that Sharpe Enterprises had sent to Sylvia, Mr Robert Baker, of Baker, Baker & Sharpe Solicitors, Chelmsford, had won the battle with technology and had emailed him a scanned copy of Jack Maddon's Will and it made very interesting reading. An idea was forming in his mind along very similar lines to Jon and Holly's and he couldn't wait to come back to work so he could contact the planning department at the local council to verify his theory. He felt a huge sense of frustration that council officers weren't in the office at that moment to put him out of his misery.

He glanced down at his watch, he was on duty again in seven hours; even though he wasn't tired logic told him he'd better get some rest. He put all his findings into a folder, including the scanned copy of the Will, and left it on the desk for Drummond to see when he got in – hopefully it would remind him to call the Chief Super and put in a request for a temporary transfer. He really needed to continue this, the excitement of the chase was growing inside him. Somewhere was the answer and somewhere along the line they would find Holly – either dead or alive.

Despite everything Holly managed to get some sleep but she woke up at 5.00am as she'd planned and lay snug and warm under the crisp lemon and lime duvet. It was still pitch black outside. She could hear the steady pattering of light rain falling against her bedroom window and knew without a shadow of a doubt that today was going to be yet another difficult day to get through. The red gleam from the numbers on the alarm clock shone out in the darkness like a beacon. It was now 5.03am. A soft light filtered underneath the door, Jon had left the kitchen light on for her in case she got hungry in the night.

She smiled to herself as she thought of Jon – he was so serious but funny and full of energy and ideas and actually not that bad looking. Sure he needed to dress a little smarter and get rid of those awful t-shirts but his hair was great and he had gorgeous brown eyes. Yes, she considered, he was actually a pretty cool geek and, apart from Georgie, he was the first person since her father had died to make her feel that she wasn't on her own any more. She thought about that fact carefully and allowed herself a wry smile. Life, she figured, was never straightforward.

Holly gazed into the darkness and wondered whether her father was nearby watching her, sometimes he seemed so close she thought that if she turned around quickly he'd be there watching her. Once, not long after he'd died she'd woken up in the middle of the night and her heart had turned over – he was there sitting at the foot of her bed, he'd blown her a kiss and smiled. I love you, he'd said. 'I love you too' she had whispered to him.

She turned on the small lamp on the bedside, pulled back the duvet and got out of bed, padding quietly to the bathroom. She opened the cabinet and got out a sharp pair of scissors she'd hidden there the previous evening. "Okay, here goes." She looked directly into the mirror and took a hank of hair – just above shoulder level should do... and cut cleanly. Five minutes later most of her hair was lying on the tiled floor. As she bent down to clear it up she hesitated, her dad had always said her hair was gorgeous, just like her mum's. She put it firmly in the bin, this would be the start of her new image and anyway it would grow again.

# UNLUCKY DIP

She studied herself in the mirror, then put some gel on her hair and spiked it a little; not bad and it made her look a little older. She dressed quickly, pulling on Alex's jeans, a soft pink jumper, a warm jacket and a pair of trainers and then walked over to the bed and pulled up a corner of the mattress. She felt underneath and brought out the photo she'd taken from the flat. She looked at it silently before slipping it into an inside jacket pocket and glancing at the clock – 5.17am. She had to leave as soon as possible in case Jon woke up. The room was silent. She left the bedside light on and made her way to the door.

Domino was sitting waiting in the corridor and she bent down to scratch his ears. "Ssh! Don't tell me you're hungry again!" she whispered. Domino looked as though he was about to answer and she waved her hands. "Okay, okay, I'll feed you but just be quiet." She tiptoed down the corridor with Domino softly padding behind her. A few minutes later he was washing himself in satisfied way and Holly was swiftly writing a note to Jon.

*Hi – I'm sorry to leave without saying goodbye, but while I'm here you could be in danger so I'm going to go and sort this out myself. And don't worry, I can take care of myself. I've borrowed some money, I'm really sorry - I promise I'll pay you back. You've been brilliant – I'll be in touch as soon as poss. Holly xxx*

She put a couple of cans of drink and some cake in her bag before tiptoeing to the front door. She unlocked it slowly trying not to make a noise and then closed it quietly behind her. She was outside. The time was 5.30am exactly.

Domino glared at the closed door. Darn it, now he'd been woken up and had eaten some breakfast he needed to go out. He turned and padded through to Jon's room, he knew Jon wouldn't be happy but he had no choice but to wake him up...

Sylvia was also wide awake at 5.30am staring up at

the ceiling. Although she was comfortable she couldn't sleep, she was too excited, she'd thought of a way around the whole problem. She was still Mrs Maddon and surely that meant that legally she controlled everything belonging to Holly because Holly was still under age? Even if the body wasn't found in time it wouldn't matter, everything was hers anyway, she could have the land, use her power of attorney rights to sell it to Sharpe Enterprises who would then sell it for millions to Ladyluck Corporation. Easy. My God it was so easy, why had she been worried?

She looked at her mobile lying on the bedside cabinet for the millionth time. She couldn't phone Mark yet, he was always so adamant about maintaining a routine and simply refused point blank to answer a phone before 8am. She remembered last Christmas when she'd snuck down early to call him to wish him happy Christmas and the telling off she'd had to endure for having disturbed him. She listened to the rain falling softly outside – another dismal day stuck in the flat on her own.

She switched on the bedside lamp, got out of bed and made her way to the kitchen to put on some coffee. However, half way down the corridor she stopped in her tracks as a thought dropped into place and she frowned. Holly's bedroom. There'd been something wrong, out of place, when she'd gone in there last night... The photograph! The photo of Holly with her parents... Her heart sank and she turned around slowly, oh my God – the photograph – she couldn't remember seeing it.

Sylvia raced along the corridor to Holly's room, flung open the door and ran to the bed. The pillow was still on the desk where she'd thrown it, but the photograph... there was no sign of the photograph. She dropped to her knees and scrambled about on the floor, first feeling underneath the bed and then tipping up the mattress. It had gone. She sat still and the room closed in on her. Someone had been in here.

Who? Who would take the photo? Her right eye started to twitch nervously and she raised a hand to try and stop it. Think Sylvia, think! The last time she'd seen the photo the policeman was looking at it but he hadn't taken it, he'd placed it back carefully. Who could have taken it? Someone had been in the flat! The tic became faster.

She got to her feet unsteadily and wandered aimlessly out of the bedroom into the living room and sat down heavily on the sofa.

From the street below Vincent was leaning against the side of the car, the collar of his jacket turned up against the light drizzle and, like a terrier with the scent, watching with keen interest as first one light was turned on then another and another. Something was happening in there. "Hey Kev, wake up," he whispered loudly. Kevin was lying on the back seat fast asleep but was awake in an instant. "Something's happenin Kev..."

There was a beep from an electronic box. "Hey, she's ringing someone, give me the ear thing will youse?" Kev silently handed him an ear piece. "Damn, she didn't finish dialling. We'll wait, something's happenin I can feel it Kev I can feel it. Hey – you got any cawfee?"

Kevin considered, he was picking up on Vincent's accent but it was taking him time, at first he thought he was speaking a foreign language and had only just twigged that cawfee was coffee. He brought out a large flask and poured some coffee into the plastic top. Vincent took a sip and spat it out. "You Brits," he said, "this tastes like crap, you don't know nothin about decent cawfee. Go get some – there's got to be some place open and don't come back without none."

Kev obediently opened the door and lumbered down the road in search of cawfee while Vincent's bright eyes continued to monitor what was going on in Flat 15.

Sylvia put the phone down, uncertain whether or not to defy Mark's instructions about calling before 8.00am. But surely this was an emergency? But what could he do from Essex? He was always the clever one though, he'd think of something. Her eye started to twitch again. Damn. She made her way out to the kitchen to make some coffee and try to figure out what she was going to do.

Detective Inspector Drummond was fast asleep and snoring like a trooper. Over the years his wife had become used to the rhythm of the rumble and sometimes even panicked when he didn't snore, often feeling the need to prod him to check he was still alive. And, like most men he was oblivious to any loud background noise when he was asleep, for example, his kids coming in and crashing their way up the stairs in the small hours, or the annoying shrill tone of the phone when it rang....

Mrs Drummond took a little bit of pleasure in waking Drummond up. He'd been in late last night despite his promises, he'd forgotten the Chinese and now she'd been woken up from a great dream involving Johnny Depp in the early hours of the morning. "For you," she said handing him the phone.

Drummond wasn't good in the morning and didn't sit up, just slapped the phone to the ear that wasn't lying on the pillow.

"Yes?"

"Detective Inspector Drummond?" queried a young voice.

He sat up quickly – this was someone he didn't know. "Who is this?" he asked.

"Ah, my name is Jon," said the voice. "I'm a friend of Holly Maddon and I'm afraid she's in trouble. Look, I know it's early but can you meet me? I'm in Henley. I can meet you on the north side of the bridge along the bank – do you know where I mean?"

"Yes, yes I know it. And yes, I can make it – I'll be about 20 minutes." There was silence on the other end of the phone. "... are you okay Jon?"

"Yes," said the voice quietly. "I'll see you there."

Drummond put down the phone. His wife immediately picked it up and pressed the dial tone "You'll be calling Axler I guess?" she said knowingly.

It seemed to Axler that he'd only just closed his eyes when his mother roughly woke him up and handed him his mobile. "Been going off for ages," she complained. "Get your friends to call you at a more suitable hour will you? I've got a full day's work ahead of me and can do without getting up at his hour." She pulled her dressing gown around her and slammed the door behind her as she left.

Axler knew who it was immediately. "Sir?"

"Get dressed Axler, I'll pick you up in ten. Wear civilian."

Axler was washed, dressed and ready in five minutes and paced up and down the street outside his house impatiently. The early morning was raw and damp and Drummond could see the young constable easily as he approached and smiled, he really was keen.

As he drove towards Henley Drummond told him about Jon's call, and in turn Axler briefed Drummond in full about Maddon's Will, Ladyluck Corporation and his theory about the land. Drummond soaked it in. "Sounds like something out of a novel."

Axler was crushed. "Yes, yes I suppose it does Sir."

"But a damn good novel you know and there's no reason to suppose you're wrong. Let's see what this young man has to say, maybe he can fill in the missing pieces eh? Good work Axler, good work. Lateral thinking - that's what I like."

As they approached the bridge they scanned the area eagerly. "There he is Axler." A young man was pacing up and down the pavement that ran alongside the Thames.  They pulled up smoothly and got out of the car.

Jon turned around and saw them approaching.  He stood up straight and watched them, trying to assess them, weighing up whether or not he could trust them.  Drummond's face was shadowed and crumpled as though he hadn't slept for days, he wore a shabby raincoat and looked as old as the hills.  Axler, by contrast, was a lot younger, energetic and enthusiastic, his clothes were quite trendy and he was tall and well built like a rugby player.  Despite their vastly different appearances they both gave out a feeling of security and Jon felt himself relax.

Drummond meanwhile had summed Jon up in an instant, about the same age as his own boy, honest and intelligent, one of the good ones.  "Jon?" he offered his hand.

"Yes, hi, I'm Jon."  Jon shook Drummond's hand firmly.  "Thanks for coming, I'm err, sorry about calling so early in the morning."

"You have some news about Holly Maddon?"

Jon pushed his hands down into his pockets and wondered where on earth he should begin.

"Is she alive Jon?" asked Drummond.

"I hope so," said Jon.  "I really, really hope so..."

Drummond drove and Axler sat with Jon in the back seat.

Jon was frustrated and angry with himself.  Nothing had prepared him for the shock of finding Holly's note but neither could he have anticipated that the thought of her out there alone would fill him with such terror.  Like a nightmare her words "if the opportunity comes along I'd like to take her out myself" kept playing over and over again in his mind.  For once he thought of the consequences and knew that no matter how good his computer skills were the police had far more resources at their fingertips and so common sense had prevailed, he'd resigned himself to getting into trouble and had called Drummond.

As he sat in the back of the car with Axler next to him Jon urgently and precisely outlined what had happened since he'd pulled Holly out of the Thames and why, exactly, he thought she was now once again in danger. Neither Drummond nor Axler interrupted him and neither did they reprimand in any way, there was simply no point - they both knew from the way Jon was speaking he was very aware that some of the decisions he'd made had not necessarily been the best. However, everything Jon said confirmed what Axler had discovered and what had seemed like a novel was becoming very, very real.

Drummond knew the chances were that Jon was right, that Holly had probably gone to challenge Sylvia and although he didn't show it, he was worried. "Axler, how d'you fancy a bit of surveillance?"

"Er, I'm on duty in an hour or so Sir, Sergeant Wells is expecting me in."

"Leave that with me. I'm going to drop you off about street away from Sylvia's flat. Get yourself a coffee, newspaper, whatever and walk there slowly. Take your time, observe, don't go rushing in, there could be others watching. I need to go to the office, make a few phone calls and brief a few people, I'll be in touch as soon as possible. Jon, you're to come with me. And Axler..."

"Sir?" Axler's face was flushed with excitement at the thought of surveillance work.

"We're dealing with murderers here, don't take any chances do you understand? Report in anything you see that could be of interest."

"Sir!" Axler practically tore open the car door to get out.

"We're not there yet Axler."

"Sorry Sir."

"How do we know that Holly isn't already at Sylvia's, that she's not lying dead in the flat?" Jon's face was a picture of misery. "This is all my fault you know."

Drummond glanced at him in the rear view mirror as he drove. "In my experience Jon, teenage girls do what they want to do no matter what you do or say. Holly was determined to do this and trust me, it wouldn't have mattered what you'd said or done, she'd have gone ahead anyway. But to reassure you, from a practical point of view, she simply hasn't had time to get from Henley to Kensington yet – public transport doesn't run that frequently this time of day."

Jon slumped back miserably in the back of the car. "Er, Inspector Drummond?"

"Yes?"

"Does my dad have to find out anything about this?"

Drummond caught Jon's eye. "What do you think?"

Jon slumped even lower in the back seat of the car. "I am just so dead."

"You may get into trouble but trust me, he'll just be glad you're okay." Jon did not look reassured.

Drummond swung the car over into a lay-by. "Ok Axler, here we are. Remember, keep a low profile and report in regularly, especially if you see Holly or there's a problem."

"Sir." Axler couldn't wait to get out of the car.

"Come and sit in the front Jon, I feel as if I'm taking you into custody. Now, can you go through everything once more just so I know I haven't missed anything. When we get back to the station I've got a few calls to make and hopefully we'll start to see some real progress. We'll find Holly, don't worry – if I know anything about teenagers she'll be okay – from my own experience I can tell you you're very resourceful lot and she's been through a lot more than most and is better able to take care of herself. Yes?"

Jon thought of Holly, how she'd come back from the brink of death, not crying or feeling sorry for herself but starving hungry and determined to find the truth. Drummond was right, she could take care of herself, why was he so worried? He drummed his fingers on the seat as he stared out at the grey streets hoping to catch sight of her.

Despite the thick jacket she was wearing, Holly was feeling the cold and she walked briskly towards Victoria coach station in an effort to keep warm. The streets were desolate and it was still dark, there were few people around and every sound echoed, the clouds were low and ominous and light rain drizzled steadily.

As she approached the ticket office she quickly rummaged in her bag, pulling out a large woolly hat which she then yanked down over her head as far as she could and still be able to see without bumping into anything.

"Return to Chelmsford, please and what time does the coach leave?" she asked politely.

"Ten past eight, bay 10." It was early in the morning and the assistant barely glanced at her as she replied. Holly quickly moved away to a bench to wait, choosing one that wasn't in view of the security cameras. God, it was cold, was there no heating? And it smelt of pee. She sighed heavily and crossed her arms tightly, she had to put up with it, she couldn't risk walking around outside now in case someone recognised her, so she opened a magazine and settled down trying to ignore the cold and the smell.

She barely read the words in front of her, she was worried about Jon and how he'd react once discovered she wasn't there, but he probably wouldn't even know she'd gone until she was on the coach. She tapped the front of the magazine anxiously, he'd automatically think that she'd be going after Sylvia and would try to find her – what if he confronted her and got hurt? But he was smart and wouldn't do that on his own, surely? She rolled her eyes heavenwards

– but then he was a boy and who knew what he was capable of?

It would take him some time to realise it was actually Mark she was going to find, but to her it was obvious – Mark was the one who was behind all this. This remote person she'd never even seen had somehow found out about some stupid bit of land and then had sat down and worked out how to get it in cold blood, deliberately using Sylvia to lure her father. Sylvia was a monster but she wasn't clever enough to have thought of all this.

Holly's plan was to find Mark and challenge him; she'd call his bluff and tell him she knew all about the land and his plan and that she'd already sent the information to the police. She needed to know the absolute truth - had they really set the trap two years ago? Did they actually set out with intent to kill her and her dad? The one thing she had on her side was overwhelming anger, they'd destroyed her life, taken her to the brink of death and if there was one thing she'd learned it was that she wasn't scared of anything, there was nothing more they could do to hurt her. Now it was their turn.

At eight o'clock on the button Sylvia took a deep breath and rang Mark. She'd been pacing about the flat for over two hours, the twitch in her eye hadn't gone away but she knew she needed to be in control when she spoke to him. The phone shook in her hand. It rang the other end, once, twice... "Hello?" His voice melted her knees and she sat down.

"Hi, Mark."

"Have they found her?"

Control, she had to be in control. "No, nothing, just needed to talk to you. I had an idea..."

He was obviously having a drink of some kind, she could hear him taking a sip. "Well?"

"Look, although the land was left to Holly she's not legally an adult until she's eighteen and as her guardian I have Power of Attorney so it doesn't matter whether or not she's found, we can go ahead with this deal surely?"

There was silence on the other end of the phone. "Yes...." he was obviously thinking this through. "Yes, that sounds logical, you could be right. Listen I'll call dad, get some advice, see if we can go ahead with this."

"Do you have to? You know what he's like sometimes..."

Mark reply was quick, imperious. "I know how to handle him."

There was a pause. "Mark?" she said, tapping her teeth with her fingers.

He was instantly alert at the sound. "What?"

Damn, she could hardly see out of her eye it was twitching so much, he'd hate it if he knew someone had been in the flat, he wouldn't believe her and then he'd yell and tell her she was stupid. A decision was made in a split second. "Nothing, Mark, nothing... I'll wait to hear from you."

Sylvia was drained, exhausted. Someone had been in the flat, she wasn't safe but she couldn't tell anyone. A thought struck her, did they leave a bug anywhere? What about the phones? She could feel the four walls close in on her – she was so near to the jackpot, she mustn't lose it, she had to keep control for a bit longer. The phone rang and she screamed.

As she answered her heart was in her mouth and she was shaking.

"Mrs Maddon?" came a deep voice.

"Yes?" That ugly policeman again.

"Sorry to trouble you so early in the morning but I've just come on duty and I wanted to double check you were alright. I'm afraid there's still no news of Holly."

"Really? I'm just getting so desperate now, I need to know whether she's alive or not Inspector Drummond. What exactly is being done? My nerves are on edge not knowing, I can't sleep..." Sylvia's voice was high.

On the other end of the phone Drummond raised his eyebrows, she sounded sincere, almost as though she really cared about Holly. "I'm sorry Mrs Maddon, I can quite understand how you feel. As you're aware, the search has been scaled down but I don't want you to think it has put it to one side – finding Holly is my number one priority, I promise you."

Sylvia was tapping her front teeth hard. "Please, please do everything you can Inspector Drummond - I need to know."

"Do you need any help Mrs Maddon? We have officers who are trained to support families in this kind of situation, you could find it very helpful to talk to someone..."

"No, no, I don't need any help I just need Holly."

Drummond sighed sympathetically. "I understand Mrs Maddon, and I promise I'll keep in regular touch. Will you be at home today?"

Sylvia looked around the empty flat and felt her heart sink. "Yes," she whispered. "I'll be here. All day."

"I'll call you. Goodbye Mrs Maddon."

She put the phone down and gazed into the middle distance. Outside she could hear the steady noise of cars and people talking and walking as the rush hour built up, life was going on as normal. She walked over and looked in the mirror to reassure herself that she was still beautiful and she pushed her hair back and smiled at her reflection. Then she walked to the kitchen, picked up the chef's knife with the sharpest blade, walked back into the living room and started to systematically search for the bug.

Drummond looked at Jon who was sitting looking impatiently at him. "I can tell you that Holly isn't with Sylvia – that's the first piece of real emotion I think

I've heard from her, she's desperate to know where Holly is."

Jon felt relief sweep over him and he slumped back in the chair. "What do we do now?"

Drummond had already spoken to several people including the Chief Superintendent, who had immediately given him official permission to do what he needed in order to pursue the enquiry, and to Sergeant Wells who was put out that one of his men had been taken away at short notice and grumbled under his breath but got on and found a replacement.

He'd also taken the time to call Jon's father, Mr Fergus McKay, who was in turn completely taken aback, worried, angry, philosophical and who was coming home on the next available flight. Jon was resigned to being grounded until he was forty at least.

"What do we do?" repeated Drummond. "Well, I do my job. In theory you're a minor and should go home and wait for your father." Jon opened his mouth in protest but Drummond held up his hand and stopped him. "However, you are the one person Holly trusts and you should be around in case something happens and we need you. Are you okay with that?"

Okay? Jon was ecstatic and couldn't hide it. "Brilliant, brilliant thanks. How can I help?"

"You hungry?"

Jon nodded, he was starving.

"Yep, me too. There's a canteen on the third floor that should be open by now – go and get us a bacon sandwich each and anything else you can find." Jon raised his eyebrows a little put out, but realised he wasn't exactly in a position to complain and he was hungry.

"I like my coffee strong and black – tell them it's for me, they'll know how to make it. Here." Drummond pushed some money across the table. "Go lad, go, I don't work well on an empty stomach and I've a lot to do."

Vincent put the ear piece down. "Y'know what Kev?" Kevin looked up. "Now that there's a lady on the edge. How'd I know? Hey, I have eight dawtas at home – hormones all over the place, you have no idea, they drive me crazy." Vincent shook his head sadly.

Kevin frowned in thought. Dawtas?

"Gyrls, I have eight gyrls, dawtas," repeated Vincent. Trouble was, no one spoke English around here. "And y'know what? Each one of them is special. Gee I miss them, they look after their old dad y'know." His bright eyes looked sad for a moment. "But anyways, I know a woman on the edge trust me and that lady is sounding pretty way out there. And y'know what else Kev?"

Kevin shook his head, he'd been lost at the first sentence. "There was something she wasn't telling that boyfriend of hers, trust me." He perked up a little. "But that cop sounded okay. Some of my best friends are cops y'know that? Keep your friends close but keep your enemies closer – some Roman guy said that and y'know what? He was right."

Kev nodded in agreement. He didn't have a clue what Vincent was going on about apart from the fact he said y'know what every few words. Vincent slapped Kevin on the shoulders. "Well, she ain't going nowhere for a while Kev and it's time we went to pick up Mr Schultz from the airport. Now he's a guy youse don't ever want to upset."

Kevin started the car while Vincent put the seat back and closed his eyes. "Wake me when we're there will youse Kev?"

Axler was sitting watching them. He'd strolled into a hotel opposite the block of flats where Sylvia lived and, like Vincent, he'd chosen somewhere that had a good view of the main door and the flat itself. He was feeling quite pleased with himself, it was warm and cosy and they served an excellent breakfast which he hoped he could claim back on expenses as it was rather expensive.

It had only taken him a couple of minutes to spot the car parked just in front of the window where he was sitting.  Although the car windows were tinted, making it impossible to see inside, the men came out to walk around regularly.  One was extremely large with cropped blond hair but the other was shorter, dark and wiry and reminded Axler of a terrier, full of nervous energy.  They drank a lot of coffee and the short one did all the talking while the big one merely seemed to grunt, it was just a shame thought Axler that he couldn't make out what was being said.  They seemed to make no effort to try to hide the fact they were waiting around and regularly glanced up at the windows of Flat 15.  Axler wrote everything down in a small notepad and then called Drummond.

"Sir?"

"Yes Axler, how are things going there?"

"Fine Sir although I haven't seen Holly at all.  Any news that end?"

"No I'm afraid not."

"We seem to have someone else watching the flat Sir – professionals I think although having said that they're not exactly trying to hide themselves."

"Really?"  Drummond seemed to perk up at this. "Tell me more Axler."

"They're in a black BMW parked opposite the flats Sir, close to where we parked on Saturday.  Two men, one seems to be the muscle, the other talks a lot.  I've taken photos of them on the mobile and will send them through, don't know how they'll come out though, there's a thick net curtain across the window... "

"Never mind, that's good – and the number plate?"

Axler gave a detailed description of the car and the men.

"Excellent work Axler."

"Hold on Sir.... yes," he leaned back in his chair as he pushed pack the net curtain and peered outside. "I'm afraid they've just left."

"Did they see you?"

"No Sir, I'm sure they didn't."

"Which direction were they headed?"

"West Sir."

"Where are you Axler?"

"Er, in a hotel... Sir, can I claim expenses for breakfast?"

Drummond laughed. "Axler, you can have whatever you want if we find Holly. Someone will come and relieve you as soon as possible and I want you back here."

"Sir, not a problem." He signalled the waitress, he'd better get some food while he still could.

It was almost midday and the old and somewhat flaky open plan office no longer seemed as quiet and depressed as it had been when they'd first arrived, in fact it began to spring to life as more people made their way in and there was a buzz in the air as phones rang and work got underway.

Jon was like a coiled spring, watching everything that was going on while Drummond was like a machine sorting efficiently and logically through the piles of information that were scattered over his desk. As well as spending a long time on the phone talking to various people, he'd ensured that photographs of Holly were sent out to all police stations throughout London and Essex and also to transport centres – someone may have seen her travelling by train, tube or bus. Jon could see that getting the balance right was incredibly difficult, if Drummond gave out too much information then the press would get wind there was something up and Sylvia would be alerted but on the other hand Holly's life was at stake and they needed to get as much information out there as possible in order to find her.

# UNLUCKY DIP

Although Drummond was obviously extremely professional Jon was still surprised when he looked up from his notes and asked. "So you're our 'French agency' then?"

Jon coloured, surprised that Drummond had found him out. What he'd done was strictly illegal and he knew he was on uncertain ground. "French agency?" he tried to sound innocent.

Drummond grinned and rubbed his stubbled chin with the palm of his hand, he hadn't exactly had time to shave before he left and already the growth was thick. "I'll let it go this time but don't do it again Jon."

Jon nodded wanly and tried to look invisible but it didn't last long, as the minutes ticked slowly by he became increasingly impatient and uptight. He asked several times if he could help but each time the answer was no. Where on earth was Holly and why wasn't he allowed to help? While Drummond was talking on the phone to someone in Chelmsford council's planning department he walked over to the whiteboard and stared intently at the weird mind map that Drummond and Axler had started the previous day, trying to see a clue or some kind of pattern. His frustration got the better of him and he picked up a marker pen, and wrote 'Where are you?!' above Holly's name. Then an idea struck him. "Can I use a computer?"

Drummond glanced up, he was on hold on the phone. "No funny business."

"No, nothing like that I promise."

"Use the one opposite, the desk is empty."

He didn't need to say any more, Jon was already sitting at the desk typing intently, completely focussed, searching for Holly's Facebook page and through that a link to Georgie – he was in luck, Georgie was on line. It took less than a heartbeat for him to start messaging her.

> Georgie? Hi u ok to talk?
> and u are?

> Jon - you dont know me but please listen – Hollys alive and I need your help

> what?!! Go away you creep!

> please let me explain!

> u don't even know her – ive heard about weirdos like u – get lost!

Jon typed more frantically, determined not to lose her:

> u went on holiday with her, u were with her when her dad died

There was a pause but then Georgie replied  > how do you know that exactly?

> she talked about you loads, please just give me 2 mins

> ok but this had better be good

Jon typed urgently trying to explain what had happened, how Sylvia had pushed Holly into the Thames and how he'd found her and taken her home.

> omg that b**** - i always knew she had it in for Holly i even told the police, i should have thrown HER off the boat when i had the chance

>  you know Drummond?? – im with him now - kinda shabby looking cop with bad raincoat and Axler younger guy

> yeah they came to our house - why didn't Holly get in touch with me to let me know she was okay??

Jon hesitated before he continued, wondering how much he should tell her – should he tell her about the land, the fact Holly's father might have been murdered?  There were things that should probably not be discussed on line.

> she didnt get in touch because she didnt want to put you in danger but now shes disappeared again and we dont know where she is.....

> if Sylvia has hurt her I'll come up there and sort her out!!!

> shes not with Sylvia but she may be hiding somewhere to try and catch her or she could be on her way to Essex we dont know - shes just vanished

> so what can I do?? I cant just sit here and do nothing!

> u can help but this has to be our thing only NO adults – can you do some networking, ask yr friends to look out for her and if they spot her to let u know – but *no one* and i mean *no one* is to contact the press - it could put her in more danger.

> its the holidays and if shes around someone will see her, leave it to me - we have a great network the adults dont have a clue about

> thnx, tell me the moment you get news, wont you – we need to find her asap

> whats your number in case yr not on line?

Jon typed quickly and also gave her Drummond's number:  > good luck Georgie

> thnx – I'll be in touch!!

Jon grinned and stretched, at last something was happening, he was pretty sure it wouldn't take long now.

Kevin stood by the side of the car and watched impassively as Schultz picked his way carefully down the narrow steps of the private jet and then met Vincent with a massive bear hug, literally picking him off the ground. They both beamed and laughed and slapped each other's shoulders and although he couldn't hear what they were saying it was obvious they knew each other very well. Schultz stood on the airport tarmac and breathed in deeply. "It's good to feel cool air Vinny – Las Vegas, it's too damn hot there, how you meant to know what season it is when you're always sweating?"

"Yeah, tell me about it," replied Vincent as they walked towards the car. "Gina – how's she doin?"

"She's good, sends her love, keeps telling me I'm too old for all this and hey, she might have something there, Vinny, I reckon this is my last job."

"She's a good gyrl your Gina but y'ain't too old Schultz, we're both in our prime."

Schultz laughed out loud and slapped Vinny's back. "Yeah, I like the sound of that - *prime*."

"So what's up Schultz?  Where we going?"

"What's the time?"

"Almost lunchtime – you want something t'eat?"

"En route my friend.  Who's this?"  They'd arrived at the car and Schultz studied Kevin carefully who immediately stood up straight and opened the door for him.  Vinny slapped Kevin's shoulder.  "This here's Kevin, he's our driver.  Good guy Schultz, good guy, don't tawk much you know."

Schultz nodded his approval and eased his bulk into the car.  "To Essex, we go to Essex, I got a job to do and then we get down to work.  Mr Henderson is here in a couple of days and we don't want to screw this up."

"Like the old days?" asked Vinny, eyes gleaming.

"Yeah, like the old days Vin..."

Holly had been weary with exhaustion when she'd finally got on the coach and had made her way to the back seat where she curled up and fell fast asleep. She didn't hear passengers getting on or off, she didn't hear the moaning about the delays due to heavy traffic, she just slept.  She was woken by the driver who was doing a last minute sweep through the coach before he parked it ready to be cleaned for its next journey.  "We're here," he gently shook her shoulder. "Last stop, Chelmsford.  Are you okay Miss?"

"Yes, yes, sorry."  Holly scrambled to her feet. "Sorry and thank you, thanks for waking me up..."  As she got off the bus she looked around, at least she was on more familiar territory now and the weather was a little better here, it still felt raw and cold but at least it wasn't raining.  She started to walk towards the town centre to find Mark's office but almost immediately felt light headed, she needed food and drink.  She kept going, she'd find somewhere once she'd located his office.

It took her about fifteen minutes to find the office of Sharpe Enterprises. It was in an old building down a narrow street that ran off the High Street and she almost walked past it. Reading the sign outside it seemed that it was only one of a number of small businesses in the building. There was a tiny café opposite and she headed right for it. As she stepped inside she hesitated, it was small and shabby and looked as though it hadn't been decorated since the seventies; brown and orange wallpaper sucked away any light that managed to filter its way in through the yellow net curtains that hung precariously in the window. She relaxed, it would be a perfect place to sit and watch, provided she didn't catch anything... She sat at a table by the window; it was covered with a stained mustard coloured plastic tablecloth and she told herself not to look too closely or to lean on it.

The waitress slowly made her way over to the table. She looked as though she'd been there since the seventies as well - dyed black hair was pulled back from a gaunt and lined face, she was stick thin, round shouldered and, frankly, the look on her face said she was doing Holly a favour just by being there. Thin eyebrows were painted on half way up her forehead giving her a surprised look and Holly found herself raising her eyebrows as well as she gave her order.

"Tea please, baked beans on toast – two slices please, and some bacon. Er, thank you." The waitress coughed and shuffled away. Holly peered out of the thick net curtains – she had a good view of the building opposite. It was almost 12 o'clock, surely Mark would come out soon for some kind of break? Her common sense told her that he would be about the same age as Sylvia, maybe a little older, and she was sure he had to be good looking because Sylvia was too vain to go for anyone ordinary. A couple of hours later, however, although some people had come and gone none of them had fitted the image she had in her mind and she was still the only customer in the café; after eating her baked beans on toast she'd gone on to drink three cans of coke and eaten several toasted tea cakes. She'd obviously made the waitress work harder than she had done for years because hostile glances were being shot regularly in her direction from under the surprised eyebrows.

Holly tapped her feet on the tacky floor below - she was desperate to go to the loo and had to make a decision quickly about whether to stay where she was or to go to his home. She rummaged in her bag and found the piece of paper with Mark's address on, he lived in a small village about five miles away so she'd have to catch another bus and then she'd have to walk for a bit. But first she really had to use the ladies...

Ten minutes later she was walking swiftly back to the bus station and then stood and waited for the bus, trying to look inconspicuous. The station was full, the school holidays had already begun and groups of teenagers were everywhere, chatting and laughing, comparing presents they'd bought, talking about concerts they were going to see and who had dumped who. She noted with interest as she watched them that she felt quite detached and remote, they were going home for tea – she was going to confront someone who'd planned her murder. A shiver ran down her spine and she sat up straight, she was not afraid, she was going to do this for her father's sake, she just had to be very, very careful.

Finally her bus pulled up and she got on and edged her way past bags of Christmas shopping to sit at the back. Forty minutes later she said thank you to the bus driver as she got off and started to walk down the quiet street. The driver didn't even glance in her direction as he pulled away. It was darker now and already the temperature was dropping, Holly put her hands in her pockets and kept her head down.

After ten minutes of walking she arrived at Mark Sharpe's house. It was a large, detached house at the end of a small cul de sac - he was obviously doing very well for himself in the property business. She stood at the imposing wrought iron gate which was flanked by two large trees. His car was in the driveway and the lights were on in the house. He was in.

Holly adjusted her woolly hat and thought about what to do next. Although her heart seemed to resound throughout her slight body her grey eyes were like flint because she was angry with herself. When she'd rehearsed this moment, it had been easy, she was going to walk up to the house, knock on the door and confront him. But now? Now she was here it was different. She looked around, there wasn't a soul about. First, perhaps she'd better have a good look at the house and see if she could see inside – maybe he wasn't on his own? She took a couple of steps into the driveway and then quickly tiptoed along the gravel path that led down the side of the house to the back garden trying not to make any sound. He was obviously very relaxed, there seemed to be no security at all, not even an automatic light or any locked gates and she walked straight into the back garden. The lawn seemed to go on forever and was surrounded by large shrubs and trees and beyond them all she could see in the half-light was countryside. She hesitated, she needed to find somewhere safe, a hiding place where she could see what was going on in the house but not be seen herself.

Light from a large downstairs window suddenly flooded the garden and she stood exposed like a deer caught in headlights and she dived unceremoniously behind a large evergreen bush. She coughed and sat upright, brushed off some dead leaves and made herself as comfortable as possible. This, she supposed, was as good as any place to wait until she decided what to do exactly, she couldn't be seen from the house but was close enough to see what was happening. She peered through the tangle of branches and leaves and started to observe; it was like watching a large television screen without the sound.

And then her heart blipped and sank as she saw him for the first time.

She studied him carefully as he paced about the living room talking animatedly into his mobile. There was no doubt about it, he was extremely fit – he looked as though he'd just stepped from the pages of a fashion magazine. She guessed he was in his mid-thirties and was about 6' tall, he had short dark hair, a strong face with chiselled features, dark eyes with high cheekbones and a firm jaw covered in designer stubble. He was casually but smartly dressed in jeans and jumper and looked as though he worked out regularly. He and Sylvia would make a handsome couple thought Holly and she shivered.

She watched him for over an hour. He walked in and out of the living room and the kitchen, obviously on edge. He made himself a drink of some kind and a sandwich and his mobile was to his ear almost constantly. He turned the television on and watched it standing up, impatient for several minutes and then turned it off and walked out of the room again. He paced to and fro, to and fro between rooms never sitting down. Holly watched carefully, not moving, something was obviously very wrong. Maybe this wasn't the time to speak to him. Mind you, she reasoned, was there ever a good time to speak to a possible murderer?

Mark came into the living room again, his jacket was now on but the mobile was still to his ear and he seemed to be shouting, obviously upset, his face no longer handsome but twisted and red. God, he was going, leaving the house, she had to make her move now. Then she heard the crack of a twig from somewhere behind her and she froze. Cats had come and gone but they hadn't made a sound, merely appeared, given her heart failure and then disappeared. She froze.

Mark stood at the window, facing the garden as he spoke. As she watched, Holly heard another crack, sharper and more metallic, come from somewhere behind her and she instinctively ducked. A red mark blossomed on Mark's forehead and he was thrown back out of sight. At the same time the window seemed to crumple and fall in on itself.

Disbelief hit her - he'd been shot! She put a hand over her mouth, stifling a scream, telling herself not to move. A couple of seconds later she heard stealthy footsteps from behind and then someone walked past her, went up to the shattered window and peered in. She peeped through the branches of the bush and although she couldn't see his face she could clearly see that he was dressed all in black and was rather chunky. She frowned in surprise, although she didn't know anything about assassins she'd always presumed they'd be on the thin side so they could run if need be. She watched silently as the rotund outline like a cold black shadow came back towards her – he'd seen her! She held her breath and squeezed her eyes tight shut, listening as his soft footsteps walked up to her hiding place. And then walked past her.

For ten full minutes she sat completely frozen, terrified and hardly daring to breathe before she crept out of her hiding place. She tiptoed up to the window and peeped in – Mark was dead, there was no doubt about that, he was spread-eagled on the carpet in a pool of his own blood. Feeling sick, she put her hands over her face and moved quickly away from the scene once more following the path around the side of the house. She felt dizzy, images of fighting for her life, of being ice cold and floating down the Thames were so clear she could feel the touch of the water; she remembered the feeling of intense aloneness. Treacherous tears filled her eyes, she wanted her life back with her father and Georgie and her friends, she wanted to be with Jon, to be secure, but no one could help her now, no one knew where she was...

# UNLUCKY DIP

As she came around the front of the house she heard a voice behind her whisper "Holly?" and as she turned around someone hit her hard on the back of her head and she fell heavily to the ground.

By mid-afternoon Jon was practically climbing the walls. Drummond and Axler had worked non-stop trying to find Holly but had come up with nothing, there hadn't been one sighting of her and, short of going out and walking the streets themselves, there was nothing else they could do.

To add to the frustration and anxiety Axler had traced the car that had been sitting outside Sylvia's flat and discovered it belonged to the Ladyluck Corporation. Although the photos he'd taken on his mobile weren't the best quality they were good enough to identify the two men, one was Vincent Merino from New York and the other was Kevin O'Malley from the East End and neither of them were men you'd like to get on the wrong side of. Vincent Merino owned and ran his own 'security' business. He had a history of gang violence and the police kept him on their radar despite the fact he claimed to be a legitimate businessman going about legitimate security business. Ladyluck Corporation used his services a lot. Unfortunately, the car they'd been using had not been seen since Axler had watched them drive away earlier that morning.

The plans had come through from the council and clearly showed that the piece of land that had been left to Holly was the only access route into the land held by Ladyluck Corporation and everyone's fears were confirmed, that Holly and her father had been deliberately targeted by Mark and Sylvia with the aim of obtaining the land for themselves and holding out for a massive pay-out from Ladyluck Corporation. Drummond waved a sheaf of files in his hand all marked Ladyluck Corporation and shook his head dourly, "Those two really don't know what they're up against... out of their league doesn't even begin to cover it..."

"Well they haven't done badly," snapped Jon impatiently, pushing back the chair as he stood up. "They've already killed one person, almost managed to do away with Holly and hey, guess what, they're still safe and sound in their homes!"

Drummond raised his eyebrows. Axler sucked in his breath and took a discrete step back but Jon didn't even notice. "Aren't you even going to get them now? There's enough evidence surely, Holly's out there, either one of them could have her, she could be hurt – dead - and we're just sitting here! And what's more these gangsters could get to them before we do and then all of them could be dead and we may never find her!!" He paced up and down in front of Drummond's desk waving his arms oblivious to the fact that the whole office had gone quiet. "Well?" he demanded. "What are you going to do?"

Axler winced and everyone held their breath. Drummond looked around the office and raised his hand, the hum of everyone going about their business immediately started up again.

"Do you want to know something Jon?" Drummond asked politely.

Jon stopped pacing and listened, his face intense.

"I agree with you." Axler visibly expelled a long breath. "We have Sylvia under surveillance and we know that Holly's not with her but you're right, we need to bring her in now, she may well have information as to Holly's whereabouts. We'll pick her up and then we'll go to pick up Mark Sharpe – local police are in the process of making their way to his house now and will hold him." He collected his files together and stood up. "Well, are you coming?"

Jon waved his hands. "Yes, yes I'm so ready let's go!" He tore out of the office into the corridor in front of Drummond and stood banging the lift button impatiently.

At the first shrill ring of the mobile Sylvia's head bobbed up like a squirrel from the innards of the settee and she scanned the room, her right eye twitching. She'd tipped the sofa over and had neatly and systematically taken it apart, tightly coiled springs to her right, stuffing to her left as she searched for the bug.

Mark - he had some news! Surely she could proclaim her power of attorney rights and everything would be okay? The knife fell to the floor and she scrambled to her feet and ran to pick up the mobile which she'd left sitting on top of the inner workings of what had been the television. "Mark?" she was breathless.

A deep voice replied and she fell silent and hung her head, pushing her hair back behind her ear as she listened to the instructions. She hadn't been expecting this call, Mark always dealt with him and that was the way she liked it. She nodded silently as she listened.

"I can't hear you," said a cold voice.

"Yes," she whispered. "Yes, I'll come, I'll be there in an hour or two."

"As soon as possible."

"Yes."

She hung up and, slipping the phone in her pocket she picked up her jacket and car keys and made her way out of the flat. She stood up straight and looked back, pushing her soft hair back off her face, at least she was getting out of the damn place. She headed for the stairs and as she turned a corner she missed Drummond's little group coming out of the lift by less than a couple of minutes.

Drummond rang the doorbell and they could hear it chime inside. There was no reply. Jon shifted from foot to foot, impatient. Axler looked at Drummond. "I'll call her Sir." He swiftly dialled her number and they leaned as one up against the door but there was no sound of a phone ringing in there. Then she answered. "Yes?"

"PC Axler ma'am." The phone shut off.

"I don't think she's in there Sir, sounded like street noises in the background."

Jon almost screamed in frustration. "Can we at least get in there to have a look?"

"Not without a warrant – but it's on its way."

On its way, on its way, Jon could feel a high tide of anger flooding through him. "Out of my way – you can arrest me if you like I don't care, I'm going in." He got a set of tools out of his pocket, walked up to the door and fiddled with the lock for a moment. The door swung open and Jon strode through. Drummond and Axler looked at each other and then walked in after him.

Jon's anger dissipated as he looked with astonishment and then awe at the living room. Drummond and Axler appeared on either side of him and there was absolute stillness in the room. Axler was the first to speak. "I think she's a little crazy Sir".

"You think?" replied Drummond.

The scene in front of them was bizarre, unlike anything they'd ever seen before – she'd obviously been busy for hours and had taken everything apart, the television, the high backed chair that Drummond had sat in, the land line phone, she'd even unscrewed the table, the legs were neatly stacked against the wall. Everything had been very painstakingly done, the settee and chair had been sliced in an orderly fashion down the sides and along the bottom and there were neat piles of various innards all over the floor as if the intention was she was just about to put it all back together. Efficient but completely barking thought Drummond. He noticed the knife lying on the floor which it looked as though it had just been thrown to one side. "It looks as though she was disturbed," he commented. "Axler, search of the rest of the flat to make sure Holly's not here."

Jon was still staring mesmerised at the scene before him when his mobile rang breaking the spell and he scrabbled about in his pocket. "Georgie? Georgie! Have you got news? What? Oh my God, you're sure? Thank you thank you, we're on our way!" He looked up at them, eyes bright with excitement. "Holly was seen in Chelmsford bus station about two or three hours ago."

Drummond felt his heart sink. "Mark Sharpe – she's gone to find him," he said.

"Georgie, I'll call you!" promised Jon as he snapped the phone shut.

They ran out of the flat and down the stairs, too impatient to wait for the lift. Thank God it's downhill thought Drummond and his raincoat flew out behind him as he took the stairs two at a time. "And Jon," he panted. "I'll overlook breaking and entering this time on top of the computer hacking and obstruction of a police investigation including not reporting a missing person *and* insubordination on condition we sit down and discuss your future career prospects when this is all over." There was no reply. "Do you hear me?"

"Loud and clear," said Jon concentrating on not hitting the walls.

Axler drove swiftly and competently through the heavy London traffic, Jon drummed his fingers on the side of the window wishing the car could go faster and Drummond was immediately on the phone to headquarters. "Find out if Sylvia Maddon has a car registered to her and if so try to track it – alert all train and bus stations as well, we need to find her immediately. And if the Essex police haven't already got to Mark Sharpe's house tell them to get a move on!"

He'd just finished speaking when the car's monitor sounded and Axler punched a button. A voice came on, the Chief Superintendent. "Drummond?"

"Sir?" Everyone in the car sat up and listened intently.

"Get to Mark Sharpe's house in Chelmsford as soon as possible. The local police are already there – he's dead. Clean shot to the head. Looks like a professional job."

Axler switched on the siren and put his foot down.

Just over an hour later Jon sat in the back of the police car, arms crossed, watching the hive of activity with a mixture of interest and anxiety. Axler had been forced to drive at snail's pace through a mass of reporters and television crews at the entrance to Mark Sharpe's house and although they were now parked out of sight Jon could still hear the media shouting, firing questions at the police as they came and went.

The house itself was lit up like a beacon against the night sky with bright lights blazing from every window and policemen and forensic crew in white overalls were like ants busily going in and out of the house. Although Drummond had been surrounded the moment he stepped out of the car he still had enough common sense to find the time to turn to Jon and bark the instruction, "Don't move!" Jon raised his eyebrows but did as he was told.

Someone else, however, did move. As he stared out of the passenger window a pink gloved hand bobbed up from nowhere, rapped quickly on the glass making him jump, then a round face with dark curls appeared and beamed at him. Jon pressed the automatic button on the side of the door and the window slowly slid down.

"You Jon?" the cheerful face asked.

"You," Jon replied, "have to be Georgie. You almost gave me heart failure."

"Sorry, had to be careful getting past all those policemen, they're not letting anyone in you know." She sounded indignant.

"Really?" The irony was heavy but lost on Georgie. "Hold on..." He opened the car door a crack and smiled, she was kneeling on the gravel driveway. "And there I was thinking you were just a very short person!"

"Oh ha ha," she crawled in and plumped herself down on the seat next to him, dusting her knees which were covered in bits of dirt and gravel.

"How did you..." he started to ask.

"...find you? Oh I heard someone say 'Mark Sharpe' on the phone just before you hung up so I looked him up in the directory," Georgie said casually. "As soon as I saw all the police I knew I was in the right place. Have you got anything to eat? And I don't think you told me everything did you? I've been friends with Holly since like forever and you have to tell me what's going on. I won't leave you know. And," she gave him the once over, "you really have to do something about that t-shirt, nobody likes Iron Maiden."

As Jon pulled his jacket tight around him he knew in that split second that Drummond was right, that teenage girls did and said what they wanted come Hell or high water - he was under siege. He almost gave a whoop of pleasure when he saw Drummond striding back to the car with Axler on his heels and he had to give him ten out of ten for composure because he didn't so much as raise an eyebrow at the sight of Georgie, he merely opened the door and commented, "Ah, Georgie, now why am I not surprised? Does your mother know you're here?"

Georgie gave a little wave and grinned widely by way of reply, curls bobbing.

"Jon," Drummond held out his mobile, "it's your father, I've updated him with what's been happening, told him you're with me and you're safe. However," he held up his hand as Jon opened his mouth to speak, "this has to be as far as it goes and I've asked for a car to take you home." He held out the phone to Jon to take but Georgie quickly intercepted it.

"Oh hi – you must be Jon's dad? I'm Georgie, uh huh yes, I'm a friend of Jon's, well Holly's really... yes, he's sitting right next to me." Jon groaned loudly and sank deep into the seat. "Look I just wanted to ask if Jon could, like, sleep over tonight, stay the evening, my mum wouldn't mind and we've got a lot to catch up on." Jon rolled his eyes. "Yes, yes I live in Essex, it's not far honest. Where are you? Driving back from Heathrow? You've been abroad? Cool. Well why don't you join us if you've already got your suitcase and stuff in the car. Please, it's Christmas we'd love to have you and then we can fill you in on what's been happening."

Drummond couldn't stop grinning. Jon was almost on the floor. "Give it here!" Jon snatched the mobile from her hand. "Dad, yes, it's me. Yep I'm okay. I'm really sorry about everything." He made a face. "Yes, sorry but loads of stuff has happened. You're on your way? Oh. What? You'll meet me at Georgie's?"

Georgie grabbed the phone back, beaming from ear to ear. "Brilliant, that's really great Mr ... er..."

"McKay," whispered Axler helpfully, a big smile on his face.

"... Mr McKay, my mum's a fantastic cook and she just loves guests, we live in Little Hambleton – it's not a big place, we're the only one with the green door on the right as you drive through, number 67. We'll be waiting for you. Bye!!" She handed back the phone to Drummond and sat back in the seat, arms folded and pleased with herself.

"The car will be here in a few minutes and it'll take you to Georgie's place by the looks of things," said Drummond.

The same thought hit Jon and Georgie together. "What did you find in the house?" they chorused then looked at each other.

"Jinx," muttered Georgie.

"Mark Sharpe and he's definitely very dead," commented Drummond.

"Holly?" asked Jon quietly.

"I'll be straight with you," replied Drummond, "it's good news and bad. We've found evidence that she was here – in the back garden, she was obviously observing Mr Sharpe – but there's no sign of her now."

"Did the murderer get her?" Georgie's brown eyes were huge, her face pale.

"Not that we're aware of," said Drummond carefully. "Look you two, I realise that telling you not to worry is useless, Holly's your friend but please leave this to us. I'm not patronising you but if it was dangerous before it's even more so now and we need to get on with the job of finding Holly and finding Mr Sharpe's killer."

There was no reply from either of them. Drummond sighed and behind him Axler frowned. "Jon, don't do anything silly – and that goes for you too Georgie. But please let me know immediately if you hear anything that could be of help, do you understand? Don't do anything on your own, this is not a game."

Jon hesitated but nodded and so did Georgie. "Will you keep us updated?" asked Jon.

Drummond nodded. "I wouldn't do anything else." A policeman materialised behind him. "Now, it's time for you go home."

Georgie and Jon climbed silently out of the car and followed the policeman as he led them away to a waiting car. Georgie looked back over her shoulder, tears in her eyes. "You promise?"

"I promise." They watched them as they got in the car and were then driven out again through the throng of reporters. "Extraordinary," commented Drummond.

"The kids?" asked Axler.

"Hmm," said Drummond. "I'm not so sure they're kids any more Axler. Yes they're impulsive and," he gave a crooked smile, "they may even have some criminal tendencies but they're highly intelligent and the way they've reacted to this situation would put many an adult that I've met to shame." There was a shout from inside the house and a couple of policemen responded and headed inside. "Now," said Drummond as he watched proceedings, "we'd better get on. Come on Axler, we've got a long night ahead of us, we'll finish up here and then go to meet Ladyluck Corporation representatives – as 'luck' would have it, they're staying in at hotel in Chelmsford."

Axler raised his eyebrows. "Chelmsford?"

"Oh yes Axler, Chelmsford." Drummond stuck his hands deep in his raincoat and headed back towards the house. "Just need to speak to the local guys and then we'll be off."

"Great Sir." Axler's face was flushed with excitement as he followed. The chase was on.

At 9.00pm exactly, Drummond wiped his shoes on the back of his trousers as he stood outside the entrance of the hotel wondering what was waiting for him inside – courtesy and lies he suspected. Axler, standing beside him, was composed. They had called at the hotel a couple of hours previously but had been informed that the Ladyluck guests had not arrived so they'd waited at the local police station and, whilst they were there, took the opportunity to go through the background files with a fine tooth comb knowing they weren't up against the usual criminal type. Vincent Merino was not just any criminal, he was a craftsman, a professional in his trade who had not, to their knowledge, done anything unlawful so far. Also, he happened to have the backing of an extremely wealthy and influential businessman.

Some news of Sylvia had also come through, her car had been spotted on the M25 at one point. She'd been driving erratically and had been picked up on camera and followed for some time. She seemed to be heading in the direction of Chelmsford but once she came off the motorway onto the A12 she turned onto a minor road and they lost her. Drummond asked for a shot of the driver so he could verify it was Sylvia and not someone else and had been shocked when it came through. Beautiful, flawless Sylvia was hunched over the steering wheel, hair all over the place and seemed to be driving with only one eye open and to say that eye was gleaming maniacally was an understatement – he'd flinched when he saw it. Where was she going he wondered? There'd been no sign of her anywhere near Mark's house at all and they had no other contact addresses for her in this area. All police throughout the region were on alert but there was nothing more they could do.

As soon the receptionist from the hotel rang to let him know the Ladyluck guests had arrived, Drummond asked to be put through to their suite and spoke to Vincent Merino. He told him who he was and asked for a meeting. His request had been received with extreme politeness, of course Merino would be delighted to see him, anything to help the police and actually, by coincidence, they had only just arrived, their lawyer was with them, so why didn't Drummond join them for cawfee?

Drummond sighed heavily, rubbed his stubbled chin and looked up at the entrance to the most expensive hotel in the area which twinkled tastefully with a smattering of white lights, a token to the Christmas season; he knew he couldn't put this meeting off, every minute that passed meant Holly was deeper in danger. "Ready Axler?"

"Absolutely Sir."

They looked back at the two patrol cars filled with a mixture of uniform and plain clothes policemen and then walked in together.

Vincent Merino was, as Drummond suspected he would be, extremely courteous and both he and Axler were warmly welcomed into his private suite, offered large comfortable armchairs to sit in and were served coffee that Drummond thought was the best he'd ever tasted. Vincent was wearing a suit that would probably have cost Drummond a year's salary. Kevin O'Malley was also in an expensive suit but looked extremely uncomfortable and kept fiddling with the collar of his shirt as if he wanted to rip it off – Drummond had a feeling this was probably the first time he'd ever worn one. The lawyer was in his early thirties, pleasant but quiet and watchful.

They all sat around a low table as they sipped their coffee wondering who was going to speak first.

"So, how can I help youse gentlemen?" Vincent broke the ice.

"Ah," Drummond sat forward adjusting his raincoat a little as he did so, "there was an incident earlier this evening gentlemen concerning a Mr Sharpe, Mark Sharpe."

Vincent looked startled. "Mark Sharpe? Well, ain't that a coincidence? We're meeting Mr Sharpe tomorrow. Mr O'Malley here only spoke to him this morning to arrange it."

Kevin grunted and loosened his tie.

"Can I ask what your meeting was going to be about?"

"Y'know I don't like the sound of that 'was' Inspector Drummond, but yeah, yeah, sure, we got nothing t'hide. Mark Sharpe bawt some land on behalf of our company some, what three years ago? Just north of here. My boss is putting in a bid to build the UK's first Casino City – y'know, a mini Las Vegas, here in good old England. The deadline for the proposal is coming up we're just here to ensure there's no problems. Hey, they made a short film about it and it is fantastic – you wanna see it? Hey Mr O'Malley, set up the laptop."

Kevin made to move off the armchair but Drummond raised his hand. "No, that's alright Mr Merino, we don't need to see the film but thank you for the offer." Drummond hesitated and turned to Axler.

"Do you have the maps please Axler?"

"Sir." Axler opened a file and laid out a map squarely on the coffee table.

"You see gentlemen." Everyone leant forward and peered over the map. "This area here," Drummond pointed to a large area marked out in black, "is the area you've invested in."

"You done your homework," Vincent commented drily.

"This land right next to it," Drummond tapped the crisp paper, "is the only viable way you can access your property."

Vincent sat back in his chair and pressed his fingertips together, brown eyes shining. "I don't deny that - Mr Sharpe bawt it for us and it was something we was going to discuss tomorrow."

Drummond paused and rubbed his stubble with his hand lost in thought. He looked around and realised everyone was watching. "I apologise gentlemen, it's been a long day and I haven't had time to shave yet."

Vincent nodded sympathetically. "Y'know what? I got the same problem, don't shave and I got a beard within 24 hours – can drive a guy mad."

"Oh yes," commented Drummond. "But I'm afraid I have some bad news for you – the meeting tomorrow is cancelled. Mr Sharpe was found dead at his home earlier this afternoon."

There was a sharp intake of breath from Vincent and the lawyer sat up straight. "It gets worse though," continued Drummond. "Mr Sharpe may have been in the process of buying the adjacent land for your company but the transaction hadn't been completed."

"No!" Vincent's brown eyes were shocked. "Whose the land belong to then?" he immediately demanded then hesitated. "Sorry, I forget my manners, a man is dead... it's just I ain't met Mr Sharpe and of course I give my condolences to his family..."

"The land actually belongs to a young girl called Holly. Last Friday – her birthday, as it happens, Holly met with an accident, one she somehow managed to survive. She is, however, now missing and we think that Mr Sharpe may have had something to do with her disappearance." As Drummond spoke Axler observed the various reactions. The lawyer looked anxious, Vincent looked genuinely surprised and Kevin looked like a brick.

It was, however, the lawyer who spoke first and he was to the point. "And what does this have to do with Mr Merino exactly?"

Drummond looked him square in the eyes. "Sir, a young girl is missing maybe even abducted and we take that very seriously indeed. Mr Merino's assistant may have been one of the last people to speak to Mr Sharpe. Obviously, we can no longer speak to Mr Sharpe himself so we're looking for any clues, speaking to anyone who had any connection with him. We need every scrap of information to help us find her and we would appreciate your help in this matter."

Vincent leant forward. "Youse got a photo of the gyrl?"

Axler opened the file and handed Vincent Holly's school photo. "I got eight dawtas y'know Inspector Drummond," Vincent studied the photograph thoughtfully. "They drive me crazy but I love 'em, anything were to happen to them I don't know what I'd do." He shook his head and handed back the photo. "She's looks like a sweet gyrl, she don't deserve this and we'll do everything we can to help youse find her. Our lawyer here is at your disposal, he's the best, costs a fortune but it don't matter – you find this gyrl."

Drummond sat back, Vincent sounded sincere. "Is there anything you can tell us that could help us at this moment in time? Did Mr Sharpe mention anything in that last conversation?"

Vincent looked at Kevin who shook his head. "Sorry but it don't look like it," said Vincent and he stood up, smoothing suit into place, ending the meeting. "Now, if you'll excuse us I better break the news to my boss about the land but if we hear of anything about the gyrl we'll be in touch you have my word."

Axler gathered the papers together and put them back in the briefcase and they both stood up. Drummond held out his hand. "Nice to meet you Mr Merino. I'm sorry I didn't bring better news and great coffee by the way, it's hard to find good stuff."

Vincent shook his hand firmly and grinned widely. "You sure you not a New Yawker? There ain't nothing like a good cup of cawfee, but y'know what Inspector Drummond? It don't matter about the about the land, that's the way business goes sometimes. Part of what makes life interesting is never knowing what's going t'happen next – easy come, easy go eh?"

"Goodbye Mr Merino, Mr O'Malley."

"Goodnight Inspector I hope youse find the missing gyrl."

As the door closed behind them an adjoining door opened and Schultz stepped out, his bulk dominating the room. "Get in touch with our contact on the inside, we need know as much as they do about Holly. You," he pointed a stubby finger to the lawyer, "offer your services again, we need to get close to them."

Vincent pondered. "I don't like to see a young gyrl get mixed up in crap like this. When we find her, we make her a good offer right?"

Shultz put his arm around Vincent's shoulder. "That young girl can have anything she wants for the land - if she's alive. Now, Mr Henderson's arriving tomorrow evening and we need this sewn up. Start using every contact, chase every lead, use money – we find Holly before the cops do. We don't find her we answer to Mr Henderson and that's something I really don't want to do, not when Miami's so close I taste it. Now go you guys and come up with answers!"

Drummond and Axler walked quietly away from the hotel. "How d'you think that went then Axler?" asked Drummond.

"It was quite an experience Sir. You're right, they were well prepared but I was surprised, Merino seemed to be genuinely concerned about Holly. But then he was good, if I hadn't have seen him waiting outside Sylvia's flat with my own eyes I really would have believed he didn't know anything – all that, 'whose the land belong to then?' and 'it don't matter about the land' was pretty convincing."

"Did you notice the door off to the left?"

Axler frowned as he tried to recall the layout of the room. "Vaguely Sir, sorry."

"It was slightly ajar and the shadow behind it wasn't constant, someone else was there."

"I'll get in touch with the hotel and ask for a full list of everyone registered."

"Get someone else to do it Axler, we seem to have a whole team at our disposal now."

"Yes Sir. I presume we won't be staying here?" He nodded at the hotel.

Drummond smiled. "I'm afraid we don't exactly have the expense account for this hotel – police HQ and a couple of chairs will have to do us tonight."

Axler's face fell and Drummond slapped him on the shoulders and grinned. "It's character building Axler."

"So do you really think that one of them killed Sharpe?"

"I'll lay odds it wasn't Kevin O'Malley, he's just not quick or smart enough, breaking bones is more his style. I reckon it was Merino or a second person – whoever was behind that door perhaps?"

"Will we be able to prove it Sir?"

Drummond sighed. "We'll see what's been processed from the crime scene tomorrow morning but experience tells me these are pros and that they'll have cleaned up well. We need to concentrate on Holly at the moment. She was there, sitting behind that bush watching Mark and it could even be she was there when he was shot but what was she doing there in the first place?"

"I'd say trying to pluck up the courage to confront him, Sir."

Drummond nodded. "I think you're right Axler, really quite remarkable, I hope I get to meet her."

"But how much can she take Sir?" Axler was worried. "She's only young, her father's probably been murdered, she's almost been killed herself and now she may have witnessed another murder and if she did see who did it and it's one of those men back there then I wouldn't like to be in her shoes. Her land may be worth millions but if she saw who shot Sharpe and could put one of them away then I have a feeling her life will be disposable once again. Or do you think they've already found her and killed her?"

"Honestly, I don't know," admitted Drummond, frowning as he hunched his shoulders and pushed his hands deeper into his raincoat pockets. "My gut tells me not. They were genuinely surprised she was missing and I have a feeling that at this moment they'll be looking for her equally as hard as we are. The only thing they don't know is that she was actually in Sharpe's garden and we'll keep that to ourselves."

"Sir."

A policeman stepped out of one of the unmarked cars and opened a door. Drummond stepped in pulling his raincoat around him, it was going to be a long night.

Jon was surprised at how relaxed he was feeling under the circumstances, i.e. kidnapped in broad daylight by a bossy girl, but Georgie's home was lovely, so warm and friendly. Once her mother had recovered from the shock of seeing her daughter and a strange boy escorted home by a policeman she'd been nothing but welcoming, all beams and motherly tutting. She hadn't even been phased when Georgie announced that Jon's father may also be staying the night – spontaneity, randomness and mopping up Henry's pee on a regular basis seemed to be the order of the day in their household.

When Jon's father arrived, tense and tired, he'd been welcomed into the fold with open arms and Jon could see him visibly relax within minutes. He'd stopped off in Henley to pick up a change of clothes for Jon and had also collected Domino, who was extremely annoyed at having not been fed all day, then stuffed haphazardly into a cat basket and driven for what seemed like forever. He'd complained by meowing in a deep bass for the entire journey and Mr McKay's hands were almost claw-like from having clenched the steering wheel hard for just over two hours.

Within half an hour of his arrival, however, Mrs Langstone had served up a delicious casserole accompanied by crispy jacket potatoes and lots of fresh bread to mop up the gravy, followed by home-made apple pie and custard. Everyone was surprised at how hungry they were and the table was mostly silent as they concentrated on eating.

Jon soon appreciated the fact that Georgie's interception of Drummond's mobile and persuading his father to come along had actually helped him tremendously; he knew that if they'd been on his own his father would have been incredibly angry and certainly wouldn't have held back in telling him a few home truths. As it was, there wasn't the opportunity for a father-son 'chat' and in actual fact he seemed quite calm amidst the chaos that was Georgie's home. Mrs Langstone seemed to be in her element as well, rushing between the kitchen and the dining room, curly hair flying all over the place, her plump face flushed slightly from the heat.

After the meal they adjourned to the comfortable living room armchairs with large mugs of tea in their hands.   The top half of the Christmas tree lights twinkled randomly, Mrs Langstone had mopped up another of Henry's accidents and Domino had been let out his cat basket, eaten most of Henry's dog food before stalking up onto the back of the settee and settling down to wash himself.   Henry seemed to be hypnotised by this fascinating furry creature who he was sure was going to be his best friend, and sat on the floor looking adoringly up at him tail wagging. Domino totally ignored him.

Mr McKay started off.   "Now young man are you going to tell me exactly what's been going on while I've been away?  And I want the full version,  not the conveniently edited one."

Jon talked solidly for almost an hour filling them in on everything that had happened, with Georgie adding her own explanations at appropriate places.   Tears kept springing to Mrs Langstone's eyes as she thought about what Holly had been through and each time Mr McKay leant across and patted her hand as though he'd known her for years.  The room was silent at the end of the story.   Fat tears rolled quietly down Georgie's face and Jon's father was quiet as he took on the full impact of what had happened and how his son had handled himself.

Then Georgie excused herself and raced upstairs but was down a second later with a photograph album in her hand.  She sat on the arm of Jon's armchair and opened the album slowly. "This is Holly, see.  And this is me – that was our first day at school, I remember I was really self-conscious because I had no front teeth."   And so they sat together in the small living room all bound together by Holly while Georgie reminisced and cried and her mum hugged her.  At the end Georgie looked up, her eyes red rimmed and brimming with tears but her round face determined. "I'm going to find Holly you know – she can't leave me, she just can't, I have to know where she is, she's not going to disappear forever. I can't have her lost."

Jon took her hand and held it tight. "We found her once Georgie, we'll find her again, I promise, and Christmas Day we'll be sitting here having Christmas lunch together ... er, if that's okay with you Mrs Langstone, that is..."

Mrs Langstone nodded and smiled, of course it was okay, everyone was welcome in her home.

The room was in darkness although a low light flickered under the doorway. Holly lay on top of the bed, still unconscious, her hair was rumpled badly where a rough dressing had been made to the wound. She'd sleep through until morning, he'd made sure of that.

The room on the other side of the door was equally dark, the man in the armchair had turned on no lights at all. He stared into the crackling fire as he considered what to do next – he'd come this far, there was no turning back now and if he played his cards carefully he could still have it all.

In a corner behind him, next to a bookcase there was a pool of deep shadow but when the fire sparked and crackled the shine of blond hair could be seen.

# UNLUCKY DIP

## TUESDAY, 20 DECEMBER

Drummond was lying on a cracked and worn imitation leather sofa in a spare room at the local police station, staring up at the polystyrene tiles on the ceiling. He didn't notice how uncomfortable the sofa was, he was thinking. No news had come through about Sylvia, it was as if she'd vanished off the face of the earth. Nothing of any use had been found by the forensic teams so far. So what were they left with? A dead body. A hotel full of American gangsters who, he grudgingly admitted, had good taste in coffee. A missing girl. A missing woman. A plot of land potentially worth millions. They were overlooking something obvious, they had to be...

Why were the tiles moving from side to side? He frowned, disorientated then realised that Axler was shaking his elbow. "Sir. Are you okay?"

Drummond came back to reality and turned his head. "We're missing something here Axler and I'm damned if I know what it is."

Axler took a step back, his eyes registering surprise as he took in Drummond's appearance - he couldn't have slept all night. He looked like a wild man with his rumpled clothes, heavy beard growth, and black pouches under eyes that looked a million miles away. He opened his mouth then closed it. Then opened it again. "Are you up to seeing Sharpe's parents Sir? Sir?" He wasn't sure Drummond was listening to him but ploughed on nevertheless. "They were informed last night about their son's death – or rather his mother was informed, his father wasn't there, but we need to speak to them to see if they know anything about his activities."

"Axler?"

"Yes Sir?" Axler frowned.

"Have you found out yet who it was who recommended Sylvia for her job?"

"Err, no Sir, sorry Sir."

"Do it now would you? Call that partner, what was his name again – Robert Baker wasn't it?"

"It's six thirty in the morning Sir."

"I don't care if it's Christmas Day Axler, call the man and find out."

"Yes Sir."

"And Axler – you've showered and changed, how did you do that?"

"There's a gym here, Sir, with excellent shower facilities, I've got a spare razor you can use and the Sergeant has some soap, spare shirts – bits and pieces you know."

"Ah, good, I'm on my way. While you're making the call I'll have a shower and shave. And can you ask someone to rustle up some coffee for me? Strong and black."

"Yes Sir."

"Axler?"

"Thanks. You've done well, very well."

Axler smiled and exited hastily.

Jon was dreaming. Water was pouring in around him, he was drowning, struggling, fighting for his life to get to the surface. He woke up sweating and sat bolt upright, where was he? He switched the bedside lamp on and looked around, everything seemed to be an explosion of violent pink. Ah yes, he remembered, he was in Georgie's room. A movement caught his eye and he looked down. Henry was sitting there, tail wagging as enthusiastically as ever, a large puddle on the carpet beside him.

"Oh for goodness sake Henry, you could pee for England! Hold on."

It was still dark but Jon didn't switch on the lights as he went downstairs in case he woke everyone up. Domino was already awake, he'd obviously needed a light snack before breakfast and was in the kitchen munching steadily away from Henry's bowl. He didn't so much as blink as Jon stumbled around the kitchen in the dark. Eventually, Jon found some paper towels, a spray disinfectant and an empty carrier bag and trudged back upstairs. He almost bumped into Georgie who was waiting for him, arms folded.

"Oh for good grief," he hissed clutching his heart dramatically. "What is it with this family? Do you normally lie in wait at the top of stairs?"

"Don't be such a girl and give that here," commanded Georgie. "He's my dog, I'll clear up and anyway mum's been tossing and turning, I haven't had a wink of sleep." Georgie had given up her bedroom for the night to Jon and shared her mother's room while Jon's father took the smallest bedroom. They walked into her bedroom and he sat on the side of the bed and watched as she mopped up.

"Just how much do you give that dog to drink?" he asked. "He never stops peeing."

"It does get a bit wearing," she admitted as she tossed a soggy bit of kitchen towel into the carrier bag. Henry wagged his tail happily. "But," she said as she reached across and scratched his ears, "just how can you be cross with him? "

Jon looked sceptical. "Easy really. Why don't you get a cat?"

"Shhh don't listen to him Henry." She covered his ears. "He doesn't mean it."

"You didn't wake up thinking you were drowning.... Georgie?"

"Hmmm?" She threw another soggy piece of kitchen towel in the bag.

"What are we missing here?"

Georgie sat back on her heels. "I don't know. I didn't get a wink of sleep and it wasn't because of mum, not really. Where's Sylvia? Do you think she's got Holly?"

A sharp image of the living room taken carefully to pieces came all too clear to him and he sent up a prayer that Sylvia didn't have Holly. "No, I don't think so, the timing's all wrong. And I don't think the gangsters took her, I'm pretty sure they'd have persuaded her to hand over the land by now. So there's got to be someone else, someone we haven't thought of yet."

"My laptop's under the bed - you could do another trawl through and I could go through the files again..."

Jon flexed his fingers. "What are we waiting for then? I'm not a computer geek for nothing, I'll just have to start at the beginning all over again – Baker Baker & Sharpe."

Although Drummond felt a lot fresher after a hot shower, shave, a change of shirt and a large cup of strong coffee, he was also confused. "David Sharpe? David Sharpe recommended Sylvia for the job? Don't you think that's a bit odd Axler?"

Drummond's mobile rang shrilly cutting through the quiet morning air. "Jon? Good morning. What are you doing up so early?" Drummond listened carefully and repeated what Jon told him so Axler could hear. "David Sharpe, Mark's father, is also a partner in Sharpe Enterprises – a silent partner, he put up the initial investment."

Axler fidgeted from foot to foot as Drummond continued his conversation. "So he would have a vested interest in Holly selling the land... No, Jon, he's not at home at the moment we've just checked... okay... listen thanks for the information and keep me updated if you find anything else – just don't tell me how you get it will you? Pardon? Oh, no, no sign of Sylvia yet either. Right, bye and give my regards to Georgie and her mum won't you? .... Yes, I'll let you know how things are going, most definitely."

Drummond shut the mobile. "At last I think we've got something to go on. God," he grinned widely, "I sound like a bad movie. Get back in touch with Robert Baker, tell him we're getting a warrant but we'd appreciate his co-operation to search his office for any information regarding David Sharpe's involvement in

Sharpe Enterprises and we want to do it now. Ask uniform to go back to Mrs Sharpe and question her as to where, exactly her husband is and get any other background information they can. Right, Axler finally we're getting somewhere."

Jon put down the phone and looked over at Georgie perched on the end of the bed drumming her heels. "David Sharpe isn't at home apparently."

"Look, aren't we clutching a bit at straws, the man's really old and a solicitor – just because he set up the business and now isn't at home isn't a lot to go on. It's not exactly suspicious behaviour – he could be at a conference for solicitors, we don't know."

"I know, but it's the only lead we've got at the moment and we can't sit here and do nothing can we?"

Georgie nodded in agreement, neither of them were much good at sitting around and doing nothing. "It could be though," she stated after a moment's thought, "that *he's* the smart one, not Mark, that he set this up and maybe he didn't just want a cottage in the country when he retired but a Caribbean island... Is that too far-fetched? I mean he is like *really* old."

"Honestly?" asked Jon. "After these last few days I think anything is possible - any ideas I may have had about reality and how people treat each other were blown away when I fished Holly out of the Thames. Now think Georgie... if we follow this reasoning through, that David Sharpe is the brains behind all this then frankly I'm even more worried than before because this has been a long-term, strategic game and he must have planned murder from the very beginning." A shiver ran down his body as he spoke and he knew with profound clarity that he was right.

Georgie's brown eyes were round like saucers and she couldn't reply.

"We have three missing people - him, Sylvia and Holly..." Jon tried to kick his thought processes back into gear.

"And I'll bet anything," interrupted Georgie, "that if we find one we'll find all of them."

"You're right."

There was silence.

"If old Mr Sharpe and Sylvia are working together then we've got to hurry, they could already have killed her..." Georgie suddenly looked panicked.

"Try not to think about it." Jon tried to be calm as images of Holly's body floated before his eyes. "We've got to be logical here... yes, they're murderers but I reckon that if Sharpe does have Holly he'll be nice to her initially, probably try to persuade her to sell the land..." His eyes shone brightly. "The land, of course, that's it! Where'd I put my file?" He scrabbled through a pile of papers scattered on the floor next to the bed and pulled out a map. "Look!" he quickly unfolded the paper and smoothed it out, immediately going to the area marked out as belonging to Holly. "There's a building right there." He pointed to a small rectangular shape surrounded by a sparse wood. Where would be a better place to take her? Show her the land and try to convince her to sell it to him..."

Georgie screwed up her eyes and looked closely. "You could be right," she said decisively, "but we need to get there and have a look - it's the only lead we've got and I really can't sit here and wait for everyone to wake up - Holly could be being murdered right now!"

Jon sighed and combed his fingers through his hair. "Well I'm not getting my dad up, he'll just tell us not to interfere and to let the police do their job and what if we're wrong? We'd have dad *and* Drummond angry."

"We could wake mum, she's good about this sort of thing," commented Georgie.

"She'd probably bake us a pie."

"Hey, don't you be rude about my mum!" Georgie elbowed him in his ribs. "She bakes great pies."

"Sorry, I didn't mean that... Listen..." Jon pushed his hair back off his face and sat up... "I've got an idea, but I promise you we're going to get into trouble."

"What?" Georgie's eyes gleamed.

"I can drive you know, I've had loads of lessons from dad – I don't have my licence yet, of course, but I'm not bad – I could take his car, it's easy to drive and it's got satnav."

Georgie jumped off the end of the bed. "Oh my God, well what are we waiting for? Come on we've at least got to give it a go." She pulled his arm. "Come on!"

"We should write a note at least," commented Jon.

"I'll do it," said Georgie stepping over a now sleeping Henry to grab a pink notepad from her bedside table. "Here we go... *'Dear mum and Mr McKay, Jon and I have just gone out for a while, don't worry, just give us a call when you wake up :o) – G XXXXX'.* How's that? Oh, hold on. *'Don't worry we've taken something to eat'.*"

"It'll do," grinned Jon, "but I think we'd both better put some proper clothes on – that pink pyjama thing you're wearing won't keep you warm".

Georgie coloured. "Well turn around a minute while I get changed and you'd better put something decent on as well, preferably hiding that t-shirt of yours or I'll have nightmares all day."

Five minutes later they were ready. "You ready?" Jon asked.

"As I'll ever be, now we'd better get going before they wake up."

Schultz's large face was like stone as looked up at Vinnie. "Tell me that again will you Vin?"

Vinnie stood in front of him, his restless body uncomfortable. "Our police informant tells us the gyrl Holly was in the garden Schultz - she must have been there when youse arrived. They think she saw Sharpe get wasted."

# UNLUCKY DIP

Schultz could feel Florida and the beach house slipping away from him, Gina would find someone else to share the margaritas with and he'd be behind bars never to be let out again. What a stupid and unforgivable mistake – he'd entered from the fields behind the back garden and had waited patiently for almost half an hour, he hadn't seen the girl, simply hadn't seen her. What kind of assassin overlooks another person a few yards away from them? A pretty crap assassin, that's who...

He hung his head slightly and his eyes took on a faraway look - he wouldn't end up in jail, Mr Henderson simply wouldn't allow his company to be publicly tarnished like that, no, he'd simply be taken out. Still, he reasoned, it would probably be someone like Vinnie who would do it, a pal who'd at least get it over with quickly and quietly.

Vinnie knew exactly what was going through his mind and was sympathetic.

"Hey, y'don't know she saw you. I'm bettin she had her eyes closed."

Schultz pulled himself together. "The deal Vinnie, the deal is what's important for Mr Henderson so we focus on that. We find the girl, do the deal and after that whatever happens, happens."

Vinnie considered. Schultz was a good guy, loyal to Max Henderson and his family would be looked after once he was gone – Henderson was nothing if not fair. "Okay boss. Let's do this eh? Now, we been doing some digging and it seems like Sharpe's father may also be in on this..."

The distinct aroma of fried bacon woke Holly up. She lay perfectly still for a moment before sitting up and looking around. It was pitch black and she couldn't see a thing, where was she? She reached up and felt the back of her head which was tender, there was some kind of dressing there.

There was a sudden knock on the door and she jumped. A male voice she didn't know asked politely, "Holly are you awake?" Then the door opened a crack and a head peeped around, the light was behind him so she could see him clearly.

"Who are you?" she asked trying not to sound scared.

A middle aged man, tall and skinny with stopped shoulders and light, floppy fair hair stepped into the room. He looked like a professor of some kind, dressed in a tweed jacket that had seen better days, and brown corduroy trousers. He seemed familiar somehow.

"Look, I'm sorry Holly, you don't have to worry, really." His voice was deep and refined, a complete contrast to the dotty professor image he portrayed on the outside but she shivered as déjà vu hit her – hadn't she heard that phrase just a couple of days ago?

"Did you knock me out?" she backed up along the bed against the headboard.

The man looked uncomfortable. "Yes, sorry, frightfully sorry about that. I'd come to visit my son but as I got to the front door I heard a gunshot. I'll be honest, I was scared so I waited for a few minutes. I was just about to call the police when you came around the corner. I must apologise, I panicked, I thought you might alert whoever had fired the gun so I'm sorry, yes, I did hit you. I didn't mean to hurt you I promise."

"So your son is Mark?" Holly asked carefully.

"Yes, yes he is..."

"And you do know he's..." she found it difficult to say.

"...dead, yes I do. It's all over the news... he was my only son don't you know." Mr Sharpe's shoulders hunched even more and he looked really miserable as he stood there. Holly immediately felt her heart go out to him and she edged slightly forward on the bed.

"I'm really sorry," she said quietly. "I lost my father not so long ago so I know how you feel."

"I knew your father too – well, a bit, anyway," replied Sharpe, "and I was sorry to hear about his death, he was a good man. He used to come into the office a lot – married our receptionist, err... your stepmother. I've actually met you a couple of times before believe it or not – that's why I recognised you and, of course, you've been on the news." He paused and stood up straighter. "Er, do you remember me?"

Holly nodded feeling more comfortable and on firmer ground. "Yes I do remember you, I met you when I came into the office with dad just before we went on holiday last year."

"Look," said Sharpe standing up a little straighter and smiling. "If you're feeling up to it, why don't you come into the kitchen, I've made breakfast and then we can talk properly. We've both had a bit of a shock and need to sort things out."

Holly smiled back and scrambled off the bed. "Okay."

"Can't you drive any faster?" demanded Georgie.

"No, I can't go any faster," Jon reminded her for the hundredth time. "I don't want to go over the speed limit and draw attention to myself – I believe that what I'm doing is already illegal... You want to drive?"

Georgie sat back and munched on a home-made cookie. "Oh ha ha, mind you, next year I'll be able to drive and then Essex had better watch out." Jon made a mental note not to be in Essex at the time.

Holly sat and ate her way through a large plate of bacon, scrambled eggs and toast. The kitchen was quiet and Mr Sharpe didn't try to make conversation while she ate, the crackling of the fire and the clink of the knife and fork on the plate were the only sounds that filled the room. He carefully inspected her head wound apologising again and again and declared it was fine but that they'd probably better get her to a doctor at some point just to be on the safe side.

Eventually Holly pushed away her plate and reached for her mug of tea. "That was really good, thank you." She looked around at her surroundings properly for the first time. "Where are we?" she asked.

"Ah," smiled Mr Sharpe, "considering there was a mad man going around shooting at people I thought I'd better bring you somewhere safe – believe it or not this is your house and your land Holly. This little bungalow has been here for years and is used occasionally for bird watchers and such like – it's a bit basic but it's fine."

"This is mine?" Holly was confused.

"Yes, all of it – I'll show you around when you're ready."

"But how do you know it's mine?"

"My son called me yesterday and told me everything that had happened – well, almost everything, I'm pretty sure he didn't tell me the whole story... He's always been a bit of a problem don't you know, always trying to find the easy way out, looking for the pot of gold that will solve his problems... I know he is – was – my son, but there were times I wasn't terribly proud of him." He sat down on the chair opposite Holly and hung his head sadly, his thinning hair falling over his eyes. "I didn't exactly think my last memory of my son would be of an argument..." He pushed back the hair and looked up, his watery blue eyes sad.

"I'm really sorry Mr Sharpe, but I still I don't understand how is this mine?" Some voice, somewhere was telling her to be careful and she put on her baffled look.

"Of course, you wouldn't know that land had been left to you would you? I'm sorry, I'd forgotten... the last few hours haven't been easy... Your Godfather left this bit of land to you years ago, your father had legal control until you were 18."

Holly pushed her chair away from the table and walked over to the kitchen window. "Wow, so how much land is there and where are we?"

"Just to the north of Chelmsford, you have about ten acres in all, mostly scrubland and wood, not worth a great deal in the grand scheme of things but nice to have."

"Oh. This really belongs to me?" She rubbed the pane of glass with the sleeve of her pink jumper and peered out but couldn't see much at all, it was still dark and she could just see the inky black shadows of trees a few yards away.

"It certainly is young lady - all yours." Mr Sharpe replied.

Holly hesitated, unsure what to do next, she was getting mixed messages about Mr Sharpe, surely an adult would have gone to the police?  But he was right, this place probably was safe.  But it was also remote...  He'd told her that the land wasn't worth a lot when it was worth a fortune, but then maybe Mark hadn't told him everything but then again maybe he had.  He hadn't even asked what she'd been doing at Mark's house.  Her instincts were on full alert but her head was beginning to throb with the beginnings of a headache and she closed her eyes.

"Holly?"

"I think," she turned around to face him, "that as I'm feeling a bit better I'd better go to the police – I saw the man who shot your son and I'm sure I could help them catch him."

David Sharpe sat up straight.  "I say, you saw the person who did it?"

"Clear as day.  Shall we call the police?"

"There's no landline here I'm afraid and no signal for mobiles either.  Tell you what, I'll clear up and when it's a bit lighter we'll drive into Chelmsford police station."

Holly grinned brightly. "Here I'll help you, I'm feeling a lot better. If you wash I'll dry – deal?"

Mr Sharpe seemed to relax. "It's a deal."

Holly stood next to Mr Sharpe, t-towel in hand, taking the dishes as he handed them to her. Although they were making small talk her mind was racing. She glanced outside, a watery blue light was finally beginning to fill the sky. "Are there many animals around here?" she asked by way of conversation.

"A few foxes and some deer – the usual, it's pretty rural. But it's been neglected for years and needs a lot of attention. I'll show you around before we go into Chelmsford."

"I never knew about this before – it's very strange that no one told me."

He smiled as he rinsed soap suds off a mug and handed it to her. "Maybe your father wanted to surprise you? But I'm sure you'll get used to being a property owner – unless you want to sell, of course..."

She frowned. "Why would I do that?"

He handed her the last mug to dry and then tipped up the bowl, letting the water swirl away. He reached over and picked up a small towel to dry his hands. "To bring the estate up to scratch would need a lot of money, thousands and thousands of pounds, it's mostly just scrubland out there and is of no use really, not to wildlife or indeed anything else. Err, do you have any money?" He peered at her with pale eyes.

"No," she said finally admitted. "No, I really don't..."

"Then," he said crisply pulling himself up straight, "your best bet would be to sell it. You can't let the land deteriorate much more, it needs a lot of attention and a lot more money in order for it to develop. If I were you I'd sell it and take the money, let someone else have the headache of bringing it up to scratch."

Holly glanced away, she wasn't so sure about that.

"Don't worry about putting stuff away Holly," said David Sharpe standing just behind her. "I'll do it later." He flipped the t-towel and hung it over the back of a kitchen chair to dry and smiled at her before looking out of the window. "It's getting light now. What about I show you around your land – your domain eh? Then we'll go into Chelmsford. Got to face the music at some time eh?"

"Yes, yes, I guess I do Mr Sharpe. I just need the bathroom though..."

"Of course, it's on the right."

"Ok, I'll be five minutes."

"No problem, I'll listen to the news, catch up on what's happening. You take your time." He turned on the radio and settled down in an armchair that was close to the now dying fire.

Holly walked steadily out of the room into a small corridor. She looked to the left, there was a door there with a key in it. Curiosity got the better of her. Looking over her shoulder she quickly tiptoed over and quietly turned the key, opening the door a crack. The room was softly lit by a small lamp in a corner; she looked around, a small bed and nothing else, just a pile of clothes in the corner.

She looked again, it wasn't a pile of clothes ready for washing, it was a person curled up, lying very still. For one terrifying moment her heart stopped but then she took a step forward and squatted down to see who it was. Sylvia! Her blond hair was greasy and matted, fanned out on the carpet, her vacant eyes staring straight ahead. Holly put forward a trembling hand and touched Sylvia's face, her skin was still warm. She reached down and, with both hands gently picked up one of her hands, searching quickly for a pulse; she noticed that a couple of her finger nails were broken, something completely unheard of. Holly took a deep breath and tried to calm herself, to concentrate on her task. She placed two fingers on Sylvia's wrist, then she exhaled a huge sigh of relief, there was still a faint pulse, she must have been drugged. She placed

Sylvia's hand carefully back on the carpet and stood up. What was she going to do? She had to get help.

Holly tiptoed out of the room and closing the door softly behind her, turned the key and walked swiftly along the short corridor to the bathroom. She couldn't have been more than a couple of minutes in the other room, he wouldn't suspect anything just yet. She shut the door behind her, bolting it firmly then hurried over to the window and opened it wide, grateful she was in a bungalow rather than a normal house.

She scrambled up onto the window ledge, then swung her legs around so she was sitting looking out and then launched herself onto the overgrown flowerbed below. She looked around, her heart pounding in her chest, willing herself to think. The casino was being built near major routes, she couldn't be too far away from help. She spied a small track leading away from the bungalow, that was too easy, the first place he'd look once he realised she wasn't there so she ducked down and crept as quietly as possible along the side of the house under the windows – including the kitchen window.

She could now see the countryside around her in the dim beginnings of morning light. The bungalow was surrounded by bare stark trees, they looked like large twigs that had been stuck randomly into the ground and were silhouetted black against a pale grey-blue sky. Dry leaves and small branches crunched under her feet even when she tried to be still and Holly thought everything looked brittle, cold and bleak like the winter sky itself. And there was little or no cover, she had to be quick and get as much distance as possible between her and David Sharpe. She set off into the woods at a quick jog.

Axler looked worried as he put down the phone. "Sir?"

"Yes?" Drummond was flicking through what little information Robert Baker had been able to find on Sharpe Enterprises.

"That was Mr McKay on the phone."

Drummond looked up, his face a mask. "What have they done?"

Axler got up and started pacing to and fro. "Apparently they've both gone Sir. Got up early this morning and took Mr McKay's car. Oh and both their mobiles seem to be out of range." He stopped pacing. Drummond was usually a difficult person to read but Axler saw several emotions pass over his face – anger, worry and exasperation coupled with extreme frustration.

"Unless we get him first that boy is going to be a career criminal Axler, you mark my words," said Drummond. "I'm glad I'll be retiring in a few years because if he does go in the wrong direction he's going to run rings around the police force. Did Mr McKay say anything else?"

"Well Sir, it was a bit difficult to hear everything. Mrs Langstone seemed upset and it sounded as if there was some kind of cat fight going on which is odd because she only has Henry – she kept shouting out Domino – don't know what pizza's got to do with anything though Sir."

Drummond suppressed a smile, he didn't have a clue what pizza had to do with anything either but could imagine the chaos in the house especially with Georgie gone. "Mr McKay," continued Axler, "said he'd been through Jon's files and the only things he thought were missing were the maps."

The light was beginning to dawn. "Those are damn smart kids, Axler. Don't think I was that clever when I was young but then I didn't have a death wish either... Tell me, any news from Mrs Sharpe?"

Axler nodded. "Only that she has absolutely no idea where her husband is. Apparently she isn't worried in case he's had an accident, she's just extremely angry that he isn't there to help her deal with things."

"As well she might be..." murmured Drummond. "Their son is dead, he should be with her don't you think?"

"It is odd that he isn't there Sir. "

But Drummond's thoughts were already elsewhere. "If they've taken the maps Axler," he pushed his chair back and strode over to the wall to peer at the map, "then I think I know where they are. They know about David Sharpe's involvement in Sharpe Enterprises and they're not going to sit idly by all day while their friend is missing, they've gone looking for her – and him - so why not start with the place where this all began?" He pointed firmly to the land outlined in black and marked 'Holly's land'.

Axler stood by Drummond's side examining the map. "That Sir, is a complete leap of imagination and we have no facts to back it up - *they* have no facts to back it up with."

"Great, isn't it?" commented Drummond drily. "Not being hampered by any rules."

"There Sir," Axler pointed to a tiny square in the middle of a wood. "If they've gone anywhere, I'm betting that's the place – Sharpe could be trying to persuade her that the land is useless and to sell to him."

Drummond raised his eyebrows. "Another leap of imagination Axler?"

Axler looked embarrassed.

Drummond smiled. "Actually Axler, I agree with your thought processes. Now, the question is, do we go and get them? What if it's a wild goose chase?"

Axler looked at his watch. "It's still only just gone nine Sir. We could get up there and be back in under an hour – not really a problem."

Drummond grabbed his raincoat. "Then what are we waiting for?"

Holly had been jogging steadily for five minutes, dry leaves crunching beneath her feet, but there was still no sign of any road. As she scrambled over the trunk of a fallen tree she felt a pain in her side and her head began to throb. She had to find a road and get help. She stopped dead in her tracks as a deep voice resonated throughout the quiet wood, "Holly! Holly! Where are you?" Fear pulsed through her and she started to run again, more quickly, crashing her way through bushes and dodging sharply around trees.

David Sharpe narrowed cold blue eyes as he stood in the doorway and scanned the areas around the bungalow. Frustration and anger filled him. Stupid girl, running off, now he had to go and find her. He'd really believed that he'd managed to convince her that the land was worthless and had been about to embark on the next step, to get her to agree to sell the land to him – he would have convinced her that it was a perfect place for him to use as a retreat from his busy life.

Now he'd have to kill her and use Sylvia as a means of gaining control of the land.

As he turned to go back into the bungalow he smiled grimly to himself, it wouldn't take long, she didn't know the area and he did, he often came up here to shoot rabbits. She'd be trying to go for help but would be disorientated, probably end up back where she'd started. She'd made a big mistake. He walked into the kitchen and over to a large cabinet that was securely locked. He took out a key and opened the wide doors with a flourish, surveying the choice of guns displayed before him. It only took him a second to choose the double barrelled shotgun and then he closed the cabinet doors and strode back into the open again. The hunt was on.

Holly stood still and listened. All she could hear was the pounding of her heart and her gasping breath; she took a deep breath trying to still herself knowing she had to be as quiet as possible. She looked around, she still seemed to be no nearer any kind of road and the bare trees and bushes afforded little or no cover at all, she was entirely exposed and vulnerable. He'd have no trouble finding her. A voice rang clear through the woods. "Holly! Where are you? I'm not going to hurt you!" It was nearer this time. She threw herself behind a tree and pressed herself up against it praying he wouldn't see her. Then she heard firm footsteps close by. She held her breath. The footsteps paused. "Holly!" His voice was soft, reassuring.

She closed her eyes, he must be so close, just the other side of the tree. The footsteps started up again and she heard them crunch away from her. After a couple of minutes she sighed and sank down, resting her head in her hands. What was she going to do now? Above her a crow cawed and pushed itself off a top branch into the sky above, small pieces bark came scattering down around her. Yeah, great, she thought, alright for some, just fly away, easy eh? There was a fallen tree next to her and she quickly scrambled on her hands and knees across the open space to hide behind it. She waited a minute and then raised her head above the parapet. Nothing, there was nothing in sight. She blinked, if he had gone that way then she must go this way, she glanced behind her. The path seemed clear.

Holly got up and dusted down her jeans. She turned, took a deep breath and started jogging again. Despite all her efforts she heard a double clunk sound, then "Holly!" and a huge bang filled the morning air. The tree to the left of her shook with the force as the shot hit the trunk. Blind fear filled Holly. She didn't even look behind her, she ran recklessly, terrified, scrambling through the woods.

Georgie and Jon had found the entrance to the property but the gate was locked with a heavy chain and padlock. Jon was fiddling with the padlock trying to unlock it when the sound of gun fire resonated through the air. Georgie's face went white. "Hurry up Jon, she's in trouble."

"Could be someone out hunting rabbits or pheasants," he said unconvincingly as he impatiently shook the lock. The heavy chain made a brring sound as it slipped free. "Great! Come on!" He pushed the gate open. "You hold it open while I drive through."

Georgie raced around and held the gate. "Come on, come on!" she said impatiently. Jon pulled up and opened the car door. "You know," he said, "we must be the only people in the world who are going towards gun fire..."

"Just drive," said Georgie, her face anxious.

David Sharpe smirked. He'd have her soon, she was running in blind panic and didn't know where she was going. He was surprised at the buzz he got, so much better than hunting rabbits he mused as he slung the shotgun over his shoulder and strode after Holly.

Holly scrambled up a steep incline, the dry leaves dislodging, shifting under her feet making her fall and she had to use her hands to grip some scrawny roots to stop herself from slithering down to the bottom. She finally made it to the top and looked over her shoulder. There he was! For a split second they stood and stared at each other then he raised the gun to his shoulder and fired, she was outlined beautifully on the hill. As the blast went off Holly missed her footing and she fell, rolling, crashing down the other side. Over and over she tumbled, through bushes that pulled her clothes and scratched her face, until she came to the bottom. She lay winded for a moment then got to her hands and knees and started to crawl away.

"Jon!" squeaked Georgie. "It came from over there!"

Jon's face was anxious but determined. "I'm going to call Drummond."

Georgie held up her mobile. "Already tried that, there's no signal out here."

Jon parked outside a shabby looking bungalow and looked across at her. "Then we'd better get going." They set off running towards the sound of the gun shot.

Holly had managed to crawl just a few feet away and hid as best she could behind a scraggly bush. "Damn!" she muttered under her breath and tears came to her eyes, there was no way this would cover her. She inched along. There was a huge boulder over there, if she could only get behind it maybe he wouldn't see her. She glanced behind her. No sign of him yet. She hunkered down and scrabbled her way quickly across the open space to the boulder. She sat down, her knees up to her chin. Think! Think! Her hand closed around a large rock and she sat and waited.

A couple of minutes seemed an eternity. She heard the familiar crunch of footsteps but then they just disappeared. She looked around, nothing. Where had he gone? Then she heard the familiar clunk, clunk and looked up. He was standing on top of the boulder, the shotgun just feet away from her face.

David Sharpe tutted and shook his head, enjoying the moment. "Oh Holly," he said, "it could have been so different. You could have been rich beyond your wildest little dreams – all you had to do was sell me your land. Why was that so difficult?"

Holly was terrified but she stood up and took a step back. The muzzle of the gun followed her movement. "What did you do to Sylvia?" she asked.

He looked puzzled. "Sylvia? Oh – she's just drugged, she'll be alright. But you, Holly, that's a different story." He lined her up in his sights. "I kill you, Sylvia will inherit everything even without a body. She'll do what I tell her to. I'll get the land one way or another. And you, you'll stay here. No one will think to look for you here. Where would you like to be buried? Over there?" he nodded to an open area.

The rock dropped from Holly's hand and she looked desperately around but it was too late. The sound of gunfire filled the air and the birds in the trees took off into the sky cawing loudly.

Holly screamed at the top of her lungs as the shotgun went off, putting her arms up to ward off the shot and she felt the hot air of the blast singe her. But dead, she wasn't dead - she opened her eyes, he'd missed! She looked up to see David Sharpe's lanky body come hurtling towards her, crying out in surprise as he fell from the boulder, and she threw herself to one side. The shotgun flew from his hands and he lay on the ground beside her, his body twitched and then he lay still. She took a step back in disbelief. How could he have missed her?

A face, white and shocked appeared from behind the boulder. "Holly?"

Holly started to cry, huge sobs racked her small body and tears streaked her face. She sank to the ground on her knees. Georgie rushed forward and threw her arms around her, holding her tight. "Oh, Holly, my God, what did he do? Are you hurt?"

Jon walked over to where David Sharpe lay, hunkered down and prodded him with a large branch. "He's not dead," he observed more calmly than he felt. "He seems to have hit his head and knocked himself out." He picked up the shotgun. "First thing, let's get rid of this. Second, we seriously need to get out of here, I really don't want to be around when he wakes up." He looked across to Georgie who was still hugging Holly.

Holly peered over Georgie's shoulder and managed a small smile. "Jon?"

He raised his hand in greeting. "Hey there Holly, still getting into trouble I see? I hope people trying to kill you don't come in threes, I don't think my nerves could take much more."

She laughed shakily and stood up, her legs were still trembling. "You know me..." she walked over to Sharpe's body and nudged it with her shoe. "I really thought that was it," she said, her voice low.

Neither Jon nor Georgie replied, they were looking at her for the first time and both were shocked. Her face was bruised and bleeding from deep scratches, but underneath it was pure white and her grey eyes seemed huge with black smudges underneath.

"What is it about me that makes people want to kill me so badly?" Holly asked.

Jon folded his arms and considered. "Now, where would you like me to begin?" he asked.

Holly gave a small smile. "Ha ha. My God, you guys don't know how pleased I am to see you."

Georgie put her arm tight around Holly's waist. "And you don't know how pleased we are to see you! I thought you'd gone forever."

"How did you do it?" Holly pointed to Sharpe's prone body.

"Snuck up behind and whipped his legs out from under him – wasn't a great deal of time to think of anything more cunning I'm afraid," said Jon, "but it worked. Now I think we should get out of here. Georgie?" he asked. "Did you see anything we could tie him up with?"

Georgie shook her head. "No, but maybe there's something in the car or in that bungalow?"

"Hmm, personally, if we're going back to the car I think we should get out of here as quickly as possible and let Drummond deal with him – we don't know how long he's going to be out for the count."

"Good idea," said Holly, "and anyway, I've got a rotten headache."

Together they walked through the undergrowth and trees, Jon carried the shotgun rather awkwardly and Holly stumbled occasionally but Georgie was always there to stop her falling.

"Georgie, do you remember that my dad used to say about diamond days?" asked Holly.

"You bet," replied Georgie. "He was great your dad."

"I still believe in that you know, he was never wrong and sometimes I think he's so close. Diamond days are coming I can feel it – in fact if I close my eyes I can see diamonds."

"You daft thing, that's because you've been shot at, probably stars you're seeing," commented the ever practical Georgie. Holly smiled. They followed the small path that wound its way through the trees to the bungalow where the car had been hastily parked. Jon threw the shotgun down on the ground and tossed the car keys to Georgie. "If you two get in, I just have to do something." He disappeared down the side of the building.

"Come on Holly," said Georgie, "we're almost home and dry now." She looked up. "Oh my God, what now? Who are they?"

Holly looked up. Three men were walking towards them. The youngest was tall and muscular with cropped blond hair, the second was shorter but was built like an ox and wearing a suit that seemed to be too tight for him, the third man was small and wiry with black hair. The three of them stared at Georgie and Holly who had  stopped dead in their tracks. "Yeah, you know I really don't like the look of this," said Georgie quietly. "I vote we go to the house and lock ourselves in. Now turn around Holly."

As they turned, Jon came crashing towards them arms waving like windmills. "Run guys! Run!!"

"Jon!" screamed out Georgie. "Stop!"

Jon saw the men ahead, skidded to a halt and then backed up to the girls. "Our plan," said Georgie, "was to go to the house, lock ourselves in and pray – that okay with you?"

"Okay with me," said Jon, "but we'd better hurry because you'll never guess who's woken up." The three of them turned to go back to the house but David Sharpe was blocking their way, a thin trickle of blood ran down the side of his face.

"Holly, Holly," he tutted, shaking his head. "And I thought we were getting along so well."

"Ah crap," said Georgie.

"Hey!" called Vincent, waving at them. "Youse guys, stop right there."

David Sharpe looked up, seeing the men for the first time and positively bristled. "You, Sir," he addressed Vincent, "are trespassing, now get off my land."

Vincent completely ignored him and made his way towards Jon, Georgie and Holly. He was impeccably dressed in a navy suit and expensive cashmere coat, looking very out of place in the damp, grey English countryside. "Hey, you Holly?" he bent over slightly to look directly at her.

Holly nodded politely, closed her eyes and fell gently to the ground. Georgie was next to her in a split second. "Holly, oh my God, Holly!"

Vincent knelt down beside her and felt her pulse, he'd had great experience in checking whether someone was alive or not. "She's okay," he said, "her pulse is regular, but she needs a doctor. Hey, she looks pretty beat up." He held his hand up, there was a large smudge of blood on the palm. "Ok, now you tell me who hurt her?" he demanded, his brown eyes sharp with anger as he looked around the small group. "No one has the right to hurt gyrls, specially not young ones you understand me? Now tell me - who hurt her?!"

Georgie and Jon pointed at David Sharpe who took a step backwards. "And he shot at her," muttered Jon, nudging the shotgun with his foot.

"It was an accident," stammered Sharpe.

Vincent said nothing for a second but his cold eyes now took stock of Sharpe and the shotgun lying on the ground. "Kev take Holly to our car and see she's okay."

Kevin strode over and scooped up Holly as if she weighed nothing; dried leaves floated gently down. Jon stepped in front of him. "Hey, you can't take her – not without us anyway, we go with her." Georgie stepped up beside him.

Vincent turned to look at Jon properly for the first time. "And you are? This is quite a little party you got going here."

"I'm Jon, a friend of Holly's and this is Georgie."

Georgie walked in front of Kevin, blocking his way, fists clenched ready for battle, her round face fierce. "You," she commanded, "don't go anywhere with her until we know who you are."

Vincent smiled. "I like youse guys. Him," he pointed to David Sharpe, "I ain't so keen on."

David Sharpe bristled, smoothed his tweed jacket and held his chin up. "I own this land."

"No you don't!" countered Jon. "It belongs to Holly."

"Well," faltered David Sharpe. "I look after it for her. And anyway you men," he pointed a finger at Vincent and Kevin, "still haven't explained who you are."

"Ah," said Vincent politely. "I do apologise for the oversight, I am Vincent Merino and this is my colleague, Mr O'Malley," Kevin nodded. The third member of the party, the stocky man in the tight suit, seemed to have disappeared into thin air and Jon and Georgie were left wondering if they'd imagined him. "We represent Ladyluck Corporation and we're interested in purchasing this here land. Just came by to have a look around whilst it was quiet. Ironic eh?" He raised his eyebrows quizzically and rocked back on expensive heels.

David Sharpe visibly paled. "Ah, you must have been dealing with my son Mark."

Vincent smiled, showing gleaming white teeth. "So you must be Mr David Sharpe? And so like your son."

Georgie shivered when he said it, she had a feeling he wasn't paying a compliment but Sharpe didn't seem to notice. "Yes," he quickly replied, "thank you, and a great pleasure it is to welcome you here gentlemen." Sharpe was now all smiles, trying to recover lost ground. "I was err, just about to take Holly to Chelmsford hospital when these youngsters came and took her away."

"That so?" mused Vincent. "Well, lucky for youse we have a car and Kev here is going to take her to hospital. I take it you don't got no problem with that Mr Sharpe? We can talk business after."

"No," said David Sharpe a tad wearily. "I don't have no - a problem with that."

"Now," said Vincent pointing to Jon and Georgie, "youse two, now you know who we are, come with us okay?"

Jon looked over and caught Georgie's eye. He didn't see that they had a choice, their first priority was to take care of Holly and at this moment in time she needed to get to hospital and away from David Sharpe. Georgie nodded decisively and they both followed.

The straggling procession was a strange one, Vincent led the way followed by Kevin carrying Holly, followed by Jon and Georgie walking side by side and then David Sharpe who trailed a few yards behind them. As they rounded a corner Jon whistled under his breath - a black stretch limo with tinted black windows was parked along the muddy, rutted lane. If Vincent looked incongruous in the English countryside then the limo looked as out of place as if it were parked on the moon. Jon sighed, he'd always wanted to ride in one of them he just wished it wasn't under such circumstances. He opened a door and Kevin gently laid Holly in the back seat. Georgie clambered in and sat next to her, holding her hand.

"Have you got anything to eat in here?" she asked Kevin who immediately set to, showing her where all the various compartments were and what they contained.

Schultz stood beside a large tree, a few feet away from the car watching them carefully; although Holly was unconscious he couldn't risk her waking up and recognising him. He nodded briefly to Vincent who walked across to him, his face serious.

Vinnie was to the point. "It's your call y'know, you're the boss - if you're going t'do anything now's the time."

Schultz shook his head. "We get the girl to hospital, she'll be okay with a bit of rest. Mr Henderson's flying in early tomorrow morning, I'll arrange for him to meet with her and they can come to some arrangement about the land – or not. So be it. Life's life, Vin - I screwed up this time but that's the way it goes sometimes."

Vinnie blew hard on his hands, his warm breath like mist in the cool morning air. "You want my opinion, you made the right decision Schultz, but you need to stay outta sight just in case she wakes up and sees you, yeah? Kev and me, we can deal with this."

"I know. Now, let's get her to hospital Vin, then we need to get back here and have a word with this David Sharpe. We make sure he knows he's outta the equation." He nodded in Sharpe's direction as he spoke. Sharpe who was watching them keenly from the other side of the track smiled and waved cheerily.

"Gee, what a loser," commented Vinnie. "I am so going to make sure he don't beat up on no more gyrls."

Schultz laughed out loud and slapped him on the back. "Time to get going Vin."

Jon narrowed his eyes and tried to tune in to what the two men were saying but it was impossible although it seemed to him that Vincent seemed to be taking orders from the big guy in the tight suit. So, the big one was obviously the one in charge not Vincent, interesting. The two men both turned around at the same time and caught Jon staring at them and he felt as though he'd been lined up to be shot and he swallowed, but neither of them said anything to him as they approached. The big one got in the front passenger seat and immediately pulled across the tinted window to separate him from the passengers riding in the back.

Vincent nodded to Jon. "Time to go, get in." He peered inside the car. "Now, you guys okay? I just got to speak with Mr Sharpe here and we'll be gone."

"Oh," replied Jon, "you don't have to worry about him, he's not going anywhere. I sorted his car out." He took a greasy looking piece of engine out of his pocket and held it out. "Small," he commented, "but important."

Vincent grinned. "Y'know what, you'd like New Yawk. Okay then Kev, we can go now and come back later to tawk to Mr Sharpe. Hey!" he called over to David Sharpe. "We'll be back as soon as possible to tawk about the land, yeah?"

David Sharpe had been standing, hands in tweed jacket watching helplessly as they'd bundled into the car. The tip of his thin nose was red with cold and he was stamping his feet trying to keep them warm but hope crossed his face at Vincent's words - he could still cut a good deal for himself somehow.

Vincent swung into the back of the limo behind the driver's seat and knocked on the partition glass. "Okay Kev, let's go." They only got a hundred yards down the road however before their way was blocked by another car picking its way carefully along the lane.

"Jeez," muttered Vincent under his breath, "this is busier than Manhattan..."

"Oh my God!" squealed Georgie. "Jon, it's Inspector Drummond!"

The bonnets of the two cars were soon only a few inches apart. "Now," commented Drummond to Axler, "and there I was thinking we'd had our share of surprises. A stretch limousine in the middle of the countryside this time of the morning can only mean one thing – our American friends are here. Call for back-up will you Axler? But do it discretely, they have the advantage here," he peered at the tinted windows "– they can see us but we can't see them."

"Yes Sir," replied Axler.

Drummond got out of the car and, pulling his raincoat tight around him against the chill morning air, walked up to the limousine, but before he got there Kevin opened the driver's door and stood up, leaning one arm casually on the top of the car roof, watching them. Drummond didn't miss a beat but continued walking. One of the back passenger doors sprang open and Vincent jumped out.

"Why, Detective Inspector Drummond," he smiled. "How nice to see you again – and so bright n'early."

"Mr Merino, I could say the same. What brings you up to this neck of the woods?"

"We was just having a look around the property whilst it was quiet – early byrds and all that. Mind you," he shrugged, "it didn't turn out quite like we was expecting it..."

"Inspector Drummond!" Georgie shot out of the car and skidded to a halt just in front of him. "I'm so pleased to see you! But I'm sorry, you really have to move your car, Holly's in the back seat and she's unconscious, she's been hit on the head." She spotted Axler who'd materialised just behind Drummond. "Oh hi there PC Axler!" Axler smiled and waved.

Drummond looked at Vinnie who put up his hands as if in surrender. "Hey, I'm the good guy here, we just found them, they was in trouble."

Georgie grabbed Drummond's coat sleeve and dragged him to the back of the car. Vincent grinned as Drummond passed him, he was enjoying himself.

"Hi," said Jon from the back seat. Drummond raised his eyebrows as he sized Jon up, he was very pale and drawn but then he looked down and his heart almost stopped as he saw Holly for the first time. Her hair was shorter than her photograph and she looked tiny, fragile as she lay there. Her heart-shaped face was bruised and torn with dried, dark blood smeared over it, black smears were harsh under her eyes and, he noticed a dark powder sprinkled over her fringe and hair – gunpowder residue? He leant across and gently took one of her hands, noting as he did so that it had an ugly gash across the knuckles. She'd been through so much. He swallowed and stood up, trying to contain his anger.

"Merino?" he asked quietly. "What happened here?"

Vincent faced him, his face serious. "I understand your concern but we was literally just looking around when we came across them. Holly collapsed, Mr O'Malley here picked her up and we was just on our way to the hospital. I wouldn't hurt no gyrl."

Georgie shook Drummond's arm. "It's true," she said. "There's blood on Holly's head, she's been hit Inspector Drummond *and* shot at and we really need to get her to hospital."

Axler strode purposefully back towards the car. "I'll radio ahead Sir, get an escort to meet them half way at least and make sure she gets there as quickly as possible."

"Inspector Drummond?"

He looked down, Georgie was still there, her brown eyes urgent. "There's something else you need to know – Mr Sharpe is still at the house and he's got..."

"Oh no he ain't," commented Vincent, pointing down the muddy lane. "He's just coming... regular breakfast meeting this is turning out t'be."

David Sharpe's thin figure was making his way towards them, picking his way carefully through the mud and the puddles. He'd wiped the trickle of blood from his face and waved cheerily. "I say," he shouted, "d'you mind giving me a lift? My car seems to have broken down."

Jon coughed. Drummond glanced down but knew better than to ask. The group watched him approach. Sharpe beamed with pleasure and came to a halt by the side of the limousine. Jon stepped out and quietly shut the car door before standing solidly in front of it. Vincent did the introductions with a big grin, he was back to having fun. "Detective Inspector Drummond this is Mr Sharpe. Mr Sharpe, Detective Inspector Drummond."

David Sharpe held out his hand. "Nice to meet you, bit nippy this morning eh what?"

Drummond hesitated, disconcerted, the man was acting as if he was out for a morning stroll. "You do know your son is dead don't you?" he asked rather abruptly.

A high pitched scream ripped through the morning air and black crows in a nearby tree replied with caws as they launched themselves into the air. As one, everyone turned towards direction of the cry.

Sylvia was standing at the edge of the lane just a few feet away from the car, a large kitchen knife clenched in her hand. Her soft blond hair was matted, her trousers and top were torn and her face wild and black with dirt.

"Wow," commented Georgie unsympathetically, "does she need a shower and ton of make-up or what?" She glanced over at Jon.

"This is Sylvia then I guess," he replied. "She looked different on the television."

Drummond raised his eyebrows at their conversation but kept his eyes firmly on Sylvia.

"Noooo," Sylvia howled like a wolf and huge tears rolled down her dirty cheeks. "You, you horrible little man," she pointed the knife at Drummond. "He's dead? Mark is really dead?"

Drummond shifted uneasily and even Vincent looked a little put out at this turn of events. Axler silently and slowly opened the car door but Drummond waved his hand slightly, signalling him to stay where he was for the time being.

David Sharpe took a step forward. "Sylvia, my God, what happened to you?" he asked dramatically.

"Don't you come near me!" she screamed, specks of spittle appeared at the corner of her mouth. "You're a monster! Did you kill Mark like you tried to kill me?!" The knife slashed repeatedly through the air and Sharpe retreated swiftly.

David Sharpe held up his hands and looked anxiously at Drummond and Merino. "I don't know what she's talking about, I haven't tried to kill anyone let alone her - the woman's obviously mad."

"Inspector Drummond...." Georgie's voice was urgent but it was drowned out by Sylvia.

"Mad? Mad? I'll give you mad – look at me, just look at what you did," she sobbed hysterically. Drummond took a step towards her but she lunged towards him with the knife. "Stay away!" she screamed.

Drummond was calm. "Sylvia," he said gently. "Let me help you, we can look after you."

"What? After what she did to Holly?" said Jon. "I don't think so."

"Neh, me neither," said Georgie folding her arms.

"Hey," commented Vincent casually to Drummond as he leant against the car. "Being in Britain an all, I don't like t'interfere but if you want we can take her out – ain't no problem. Mr O'Malley here's trained y'know."

Drummond turned around decisively. "You two," he said succinctly to Jon and Georgie. "No more comments, you're not helping. You," he pointed to Vincent, "thanks for the offer but I'll deal with this."

"After you," grinned Vincent. "This is sure turning out to be an interesting morning. Be careful though,

Sharpe's right about one thing, she's nuts, ain't nothing predictable about a woman with a knife."

"Nuts?! Nuts?! And who the hell are you?" Sylvia yelled, waving the knife.

"Hey, I'm the one who ain't going to jail lady."

Sylvia backed off. "I need a car."

"You can take his," offered Georgie innocently, pointing to Sharpe. "It's back at the bungalow." Sylvia's right eye started to twitch wildly.

Drummond sighed deeply. "Look Sylvia," he said before anyone else could interrupt. "You need medical treatment, you don't look well, we'll take care of you. You need rest and a good cup of tea. We can sit down and talk about all this."

Sylvia's shoulders slumped. "Mark's really dead?" she asked. Her right eye twitched disconcertingly making it difficult for Drummond to concentrate.

"I'm sorry," he replied. "But yes, he's dead. Sylvia, enough is enough surely? Come with us."

She looked around, eye twitching, gleaming. "I will not come with you. You – all of you," she waved the knife, "are on my land, get off now, this instant."

Drummond stepped forward quickly before Jon could put in a comment. "If you won't come with me of your own accord then I'm afraid I'll have to arrest you for the attempted murder of Holly Maddon."

Sylvia's face set like a mask. "This," she said through gritted teeth, "is my land, I have power of attorney. You can't prove anything. Now go away - move! And take him with you," she pointed at Sharpe. "He drugged me, tried to kill me!" She ran forward towards Sharpe, knife raised but as she did so a hand came down hard from behind and knocked it to the ground. The same hand grabbed one wrist and then the other and pulled them both firmly behind her. Axler had handcuffs on her in a split second. "I'll kill you!" she screamed and kicked out. "Let me go! You have no right, this is my land! I haven't done anything – I'm the victim here!"

Drummond walked up to her. "On the contrary," he said speaking so softly she had to be quiet to hear him. "You almost destroyed a young life. But Holly is alive despite everything you have done to her and if I have my way you will spend a very long time in jail." He nodded to Axler. "Now please take her away will you?"

Sylvia slumped, her mouth open.

"Wait! Please..." said a young voice.

What now Drummond thought wearily, I haven't even had breakfast yet.

Holly climbed unsteadily out of the limousine. Jon and Georgie rushed to support her but she waved them away. She looked incredibly fragile as she stood there, but her jaw was set and determined. Vincent stood up straight respectfully and Drummond folded his hands in front of him watching the situation carefully as Holly walked up to Sylvia. Sylvia looked as though she'd seen a ghost, her eyes were wide, pupils dilated. Axler held Sylvia's hands firmly behind her back as Holly approached.

"Sylvia?" asked Holly.

Sylvia nodded dumbly.

"I want to ask you something." Sylvia looked around for help but none was forthcoming.

"Please bend down a bit." Sylvia bent her head slightly and Holly leant forward and whispered something to her. Sylvia stood up straight, looked down at Holly and a sneer crossed her face, she nodded yes.

Holly felt numb, as if she was the only one standing in that brown, muddy lane on a cold December morning. Her and the trees and the sky. She sighed and looked around. Diamonds. She saw the glimmer of a winter sun on the horizon and looked up and saw birds silently wheeling high above her. A single tear ran softly down her face.

Then she used all the strength she had left and swung a right hook, knocking Sylvia squarely on the chin.  The blow was surprisingly strong and Sylvia would have fallen to her knees but Axler supported her, keeping her standing up.

Georgie was by Holly's side immediately.  "Oh Holly!" she cried and hugged her tight as if she'd never let her go.

"I'm okay," came Holly's muffled voice and then she stepped back but still held onto Georgie's hand. "Hi," she said waving her fingers to Drummond and frowned, her legs were all wobbly and she didn't know why. "I'd just like to say as well that he," she pointed to Sharpe, "not only hit me on the head but he tried to kill me with a shotgun.  He shot at me three times and I'm very," her chin wobbled, "very tired of people trying to kill me."  Treacherous tears gently spilt over and ran down her face.

Vincent coughed and motioned to Kevin, who opened the car door.  "Inspector Drummond," he said politely, "we'll take Holly to the hospital and don't worry, I'll personally make sure she's okay."  He turned to look at Holly.  "I promise you no one will hurt you while I'm around, you understand?  You can trust me yeah?"

Holly's tearful but steady grey eyes measured his bright brown eyes and she nodded.

Axler led Sylvia to the car and put her unceremoniously in the back seat.  Jon caught Drummond's arm.  "Sharpe," he said, "he's trying to get away and the shotgun's back there."  Sharpe had quietly distanced himself from the group and was making his way back to the bungalow.

"Axler!  And that one too, please."

Axler grinned.  "It'll be a pleasure Sir, an absolute pleasure."

Within two minutes David Sharpe was also handcuffed and sitting next to Sylvia, his pointed nose twitching with indignation and two police motorcyclists arrived screeching to a halt in front of their car, sirens blaring.  Drummond gave them their instructions and the black limousine was soon a dot on the horizon ahead of them as it sped on its way, escorted, to the hospital.

"What a morning!" commented Drummond. "This case is one for the books. If Sharpe tried to shoot Holly, I wonder if he shot his own son? Money does do strange things." He looked around. "We'll have to cordon off this area and get forensics up here as soon as possible and Axler, radio ahead to the hospital, we'll need to test Holly and her clothes before they clean her up too much, she had gunshot residue all over her."

"Yes Sir," replied Axler. "Er, Sir, we'd better go."

"Indeed we had," Drummond got in the car, "we've got a lot to do." He frowned in thought. "So who was the man sitting in the front seat of the limousine? The windows may be tinted but there was definitely someone else there, probably the same person who didn't want to make himself known last night - have we had any reports in?"

"Schultz, I believe is his name Sir," replied Axler immediately. "One of Henderson's top guys, been working for him for over 30 years. A professional killer according to the local police – he came over by private jet yesterday - they were surprised we were enquiring, they thought he was retired but it looks as though he may have had one last job."

"The day isn't over yet then is it?" said Drummond. "As quick as you can Axler, we need to get to these two booked and secure then get to the hospital as soon as possible, it's not every day I get to interview a professional killer."

"I'll radio for surveillance to be kept on the car."

"I'll do that - you drive."

Axler nodded and put his foot down.

Jon stood at the vending machine in the hospital corridor trying to decide what to have.

"Need some money?" asked Georgie appearing beside him.

"Nope, I'd just like to be able to make a decision – I feel as though my brain's gone missing."

Georgie grinned widely. "That's boys for you, nothing new there!"

Jon stared at the bars of chocolate standing idly in neat rows. "Yep," he muttered to himself, "I guess I asked for that. You know, I'm not even sure that I'm hungry any more. How's Holly?"

"That's why I'm here, she's awake and demanding chocolate." Georgie put some coins in the machine and pressed a couple of buttons, there was whirling sound as a bar of chocolate wobbled forward and then fell to its fate.

"I really thought that was it in the car on the way here, she scared the life out of me when she passed out again," remarked Jon.

"Hey!" Georgie punched his arm. "You know yourself she's tough - little bump on the head, being shot at and almost drowned won't keep her down for long."

"Yeah, I guess. They've done all the scans and stuff now?"

"Yep but Mr Merino is arranging for her to be moved to a private hospital as soon as possible so she can recover in peace and quiet for a few days."

Jon scowled. "As if we don't know why he's got her best interests at heart."

Georgie shrugged. "I guess, but he genuinely seems to care about her as well – I mean it's not just about the land and the money. He was telling me he's got eight daughters – eight! Can you imagine? Said I reminded him of this sixth daughter... or was it seventh..."

"You do know it was probably him that shot Mark, don't you? I somehow don't think that David Sharpe would kill his own son even though he is as mad as a box of frogs."

Georgie was quiet. "Well, yes it had occurred to me. Look, I know it's probably irrational and wrong in so many ways but I'm just saying Mr Merino won't hurt Holly, he likes her and he'll take care of her and that's all I'm worried about."

Jon sat down in a chair in the corridor and leant forward, resting his arms along the length of his legs. Georgie sat down next to him. "So, how's your dad?" she asked.

"Well, despite the fact I took his car, indulged in unlawful internet activity, have broken into private property – three times now – come up against a possible murderer with a shotgun and haven't done my coursework and/or revision as promised, I actually think it'll take more time for him to recover from the car journey here with your mother – your mum is apparently quite a nippy driver."

Georgie grinned happily. "Yep, that's my mum for you!"

"Has she said anything to you?" he asked. "I've got a feeling dad would like to string me up but is holding back because we're in the hospital and there's a ton of people around, he's just waiting for the right time to pounce."

"Not so far she hasn't," replied Georgie. "But then she's pretty laid back as mums go. She's just over the moon that Holly's been found."

"Will you guys look after her now?"

"Absolutely. She'll come back and live with us.... if it's allowed that is, I'm not too sure of the formalities and all."

Jon scratched his chin. "This has been quite a rollercoaster you know. Not every day you pick a girl out of the Thames and then get caught up in murder, land deals, dodgy solicitors and gangsters..."

Georgie sighed. "It isn't over yet you know. It's going to take a long time for Holly to recover. She'll have to get through a court case, testify and everything..."

Jon sat up straight. "Just one day at a time I guess."

"Yep," Georgie waved the chocolate bar in the air, "now come on, we'd better go back and check on her otherwise she'll be complaining about the service."

Holly lay still in the hospital bed waiting for Georgie to come back. Despite the medication her body was aching all over and was feeling incredibly tired. She heard a strong American accent outside her door firmly telling someone that he was there to keep an eye on things and she smiled, Mr Merino had been as good as his word and was a very effective terrier come guard dog; personally, she liked him.

"Hey Holly," Vincent popped his head around the door. "You up to company now?"

She heard a deep sigh behind him and a man in a shabby raincoat pushed neatly past followed by a younger man, casually dressed. She frowned, trying to remember, then smiled widely.

"Holly?" asked Drummond. "I'm Detective Inspector Drummond and this," he nodded towards Axler, "is PC Axler. We haven't met each other formally but I – we, Axler and myself - have been trying to find you since the night you disappeared."

Holly sat up in bed. "Jon's told me loads about you, please sit down."

"You're not too tired?" Her face still had red welts from lacerations across it, but no stitches had been needed and the blood and dirt had been washed off. She seemed a lot better than she had done when she first came in but still looked exhausted and extremely fragile.

"Not too bad thanks," she smoothed the crisp white bed sheet and shuffled herself up into a higher sitting position.

"Your head?"

"Oh, they've said I was lucky, just a big bump and a headache but no fractures or anything like that."

"Are you up to a few questions?"

"Definitely," she replied seriously. "I'd like to get things sorted before anyone else tries to kill me."

Drummond pulled up a chair and motioned for Axler to do the same. "I can't tell you how pleased I am you're going to be okay, you've been incredibly brave and courageous beyond belief. Look, I've brought something for you." He rummaged about in the inside of his coat and handed her an envelope. "The bungalow where Sharpe kept you has been searched and your jacket found its way back to the station – I found this inside one of the pockets, I thought you'd like it."

Holly slowly opened the envelope knowing what was inside and as she took out the photograph she stroked the surface gently, she could almost touch the happiness she'd felt the day that photograph was taken. She'd giggled so much and could see everything from the top of her dad's shoulders. She remembered her mum's warm hugs and the hot chocolate she made with marshmallows on top when they got home. She wanted to be back in the photograph, to be young again and loved, so much it made her heart almost stop. Her face was bereft.

"Holly," Drummond said softly. "I'm sorry if it's upset you..."

"No, no, thank you, it's just perfect," she laid it on the bed next to her and rested her hand lightly on it, before wiping her tears away. "Tell me," she asked, "what's happened to Sylvia and Mr Sharpe."

"Axler, would you like to do the honours?"

"It would be a pleasure Sir," Axler said firmly. "But first I'd like to say myself how pleased I am you're okay Holly, you're quite remarkable."

Holly blushed.

"Right," he quickly continued, realising he'd embarrassed her. "You'll be pleased to hear that Sylvia has been charged with suspected murder, attempted murder and conspiracy and David Sharpe has been charged with attempted murder, conspiracy and kidnapping. We expect both of them to spend a very long time behind bars."

There was a commotion outside the door. "I think our peace and quiet is over Axler," said Drummond resigned as he recognised the voices.

The door burst open and in swept Georgie followed by Jon. "Inspector Drummond, PC Axler!" she said cheerily. "You're here at last - how're things? You have locked that mad woman up haven't you?"

"Oh yes," replied Drummond, "you don't have to worry about her again."

"Great," she plonked herself down on a chair. "Now tell us everything."

Axler raised his eyebrows, the room fell silent.

"Holly may want to talk privately to Inspector Drummond," said Jon.

"Really?" said Georgie surprised. "Do you Holly?" Holly looked a bit embarrassed. "Oh grief, I'm so stupid, I'm sorry, come on Jon, we'll go and find your dad, mum's talking about driving him to collect his car, he'll need all the help he can get." She handed Holly her bar of chocolate and turned to leave. "Enjoy – love you!"

"We'll see you soon," said Jon.

"Thanks," said Holly.

"Bye, c'mon Jon," ordered Georgie already half way out of the door. "Hey Mr Merino d'you want to come with us, you've been there all morning."

Drummond heard him reply, "Yeah sure, why not, could do with a break - I'm sure she'll be safe with the cops..."

The door closed and they heard the clatter of footsteps along the corridor and then it was quiet again.

"Firstly," said Drummond, "I'd like to know if you're alright with Mr Merino being here. I hear he's organising for you to go to a private hospital, are you comfortable with that? If you'd like him to leave I can arrange it without him taking offence."

Holly gave a small smile. "He's actually quite nice. I know he's got a vested interest in looking after me – his company wants the land doesn't it? – and I know he's a slightly shady character, but he makes me feel safe. I mean, I know I'm safe now, it's just that..."

"Don't worry," said Drummond, "you don't have to explain, it's no surprise at all under the circumstances, just take my advice and don't be too open with him until you're ready."

"I won't, I don't have many illusions about people left."

"No, no, I guess you don't and with every reason. But Holly, we need to talk about what happens next and if Sylvia and David Sharpe are to go behind bars you have to tell us everything that's happened," he paused. "Do you mind if Axler takes notes? He'll type them up into a statement for you to sign later." She shook her head and Axler got out a notebook. "Firstly, what happened on the riverboat last Friday? Did Sylvia try to kill you?"

"Was it only last Friday? Seems so long ago now, so much has happened..." Holly composed herself and spoke at length about what happened that night. Drummond listened quietly, only asking the occasional question and Axler wrote everything down.

"And can I ask you, what did you say to Sylvia this morning – can you tell me that?" He already knew the answer but had to hear her say it.

Holly bit her bottom lip. "I asked her if she killed my dad. She nodded yes."

Drummond looked grim. "I know this is hard, but when you're well enough, do you think you can go into a court and say that?"

"Oh yes, without a doubt," replied Holly and Drummond saw, for the first time, the glint in the grey eyes that Jon had come to know so well.

"Can I also ask," he said casually, "can you remember how many people were there with Mr Merino this morning?"

Holly frowned, thinking. "Two, yes there were two others, we just about to get into the car to get away and there they were, I think they were just as surprised as we were. There was Mr Merino and Mr O'Malley and someone else but I only caught a glimpse of him – I wasn't really myself then, my head was just hurting so much, but Jon and Georgie would definitely know."

"Ok, thanks Holly. Now, the next big question – were you actually in Mark Sharpe's garden when he was killed..."

"Mark Sharpe?" She didn't hesitate but started talking quickly. "Yes, I saw him killed. I was sitting in the middle of a large bush, just watching him, I wanted to see what he was like before I spoke to him. There was a loud crack just like in the films and then he fell over backwards, the glass just seemed to drop, I remember that."

"Did you see who shot him? Mr Sharpe seems to be under the impression that you did see who did it."

Holly's face coloured. "I'm so sorry, I told him that because I wanted a good reason to get out of the house, for him to take me to Chelmsford. I'm really sorry – am I in trouble?"

Drummond shook his head, he was disappointed but tried not to let it show. "No, you're not in trouble Holly, far from it, you were trying to save yourself – you're an extremely quick thinker. Now can you tell me exactly what happened?"

"Well, the shot came from behind me – scares me to think the guy who shot him must have been there most of the time I was. I was just sitting, hidden in a bush, and but either he didn't know I was there or he didn't care. Once he'd shot Mark he walked right past me and up to the window, he looked in, then walked back past me to the back of the garden. I remember he was large but that's all."

"By large do you mean big built or tall?"

"Definitely big built, I remember thinking that surely people who did something like that should be thin in case they had to run..."

Drummond remembered the photograph of Schultz that had come in, he had a heavy frame.

"I know you said you didn't see him clearly but do you think you'd recognise him if I were to show you some photographs?"

Holly took her time and thought deeply. "No, I'm sorry, I couldn't – it was dark, I just saw an outline and he was all in black and, to be honest, I had my eyes shut a lot of the time. When he walked past me I can't tell you how terrified I was."

Drummond sat back in the chair and disappointment showed on Axler's face. Despite the order for surveillance, Schultz had somehow managed to leave the car unnoticed at the hospital and without evidence of any kind they both knew they would not be able to bring him in for questioning.

"I'm sorry..."

"Really, it's not a problem, I'm sure forensics will find something," Drummond reassured her, "and we have Sylvia and Mr Sharpe. Are you up to knowing exactly what happened? Mr Sharpe is being extremely co-operative."

Holly nodded and relaxed back against the pillows.

"It seems that this was all, in actual fact, David Sharpe's idea from the very beginning. Apparently he'd helped your father draw up his Will some years ago and knew about the land but thought nothing of it until his son mentioned a parcel of land he was interested in buying to the north of Chelmsford. This was over a couple of years ago now. Mr Sharpe had already helped Mark set up the company Sharpe Enterprises and because of that had a vested interest in it doing well – whenever he could, he sent business his son's way.

"He thought he'd hit the jackpot when he realised that the piece of land his son so desperately wanted was owned by a client – your father. It was him, not Mark who realised the potential, that they could demand their own figure for the land from Ladyluck Corporation.

"He knew Mark's girlfriend Sylvia and suggested that she come and work at the office. He arranged for your father to come in and that was it, Sylvia did what she did best and your father was hooked. According to Mr Sharpe, the initial idea was that Sylvia persuade your father to give her the land as a gift but then Mark and Sylvia took it one step further and decided that she would marry your father, and then err..." he paused to study Holly's face, making sure he wasn't going too far but her face was set, "find the best opportunity to get rid of him. They thought that as well as the land they may as well have all his estate. It was a cold-blooded plan."

Holly was pale as a sheet. "Can I have a drink please?"

"Of course," Axler stood up. "What would you like?"

"A coke please."

"Are you alright?" asked Drummond, concerned.

She gave a small smile. "Too late Inspector Drummond, I'll never be alright, not really will I? But I promised myself I'd find out what happened to dad and now I'll make sure that Sylvia and David Sharp never hurt anyone again. It's just the way it is..."

He nodded, he understood. Axler handed her a glass and she took a sip. "Are you up to a bit more talking?"

Holly sigh but nodded. They spoke in depth for a full half hour and at the end she was exhausted but somehow felt lighter. Drummond could see her eyes closing, her hand relaxing on the photograph of her parents and nodded to Axler, it was time to go. They walked quietly out of the room and into the corridor which seemed to be crammed full of people – Jon and Georgie, Vincent and Kevin, Mr McKay and Mrs Langstone, a couple of nurses, the hospital manager and a couple of reporters from the press. He drew himself up, put his finger to his lips and pointed down the corridor. "Shhh, she's sleeping." The group tiptoed down to the end of the corridor.

You," he pointed to the reporters. "There will be a press conference called first thing tomorrow and I'll answer all your questions then, now is not appropriate." The hospital manager ushered them away.

"Mrs Langstone, I suggest you go home and that Mr McKay goes with you." Mrs Langstone nodded, she was worried about Henry, she'd left him with a neighbour and had no doubt that the neighbour would be fed up of mopping up accidents by now.

"Jon and Georgie, it's been a long day. Holly is probably going to sleep for the rest of the afternoon now so please go home, get some rest and something to eat. However," he looked over at Mrs Langstone and Mr McKay, "please can you bring them to the station sometime this afternoon, I need full statements from both of them. When they've finished they can come back to see Holly."

Jon and Georgie looked at each other but for once made no comment.

"Mr Merino," Vincent looked up, "I haven't had a decent cup of coffee all day, how about we go and find some, I'm sure Mr O'Malley will be pleased to take your place in front of Holly's door for a short time."

He looked around at the expectant faces. "Now go everyone, go!" They scattered.

"Coffee Mr Merino?"

Vincent grinned. "Cawfee it is Inspector."

Schultz undid the last button of his tight jacket,

breathing a sigh of relief as he did so. He gently eased himself into a comfortable armchair, putting a welcome bottle of cold beer to his lips. The afternoon light had long since faded but he hadn't turned on the lights in the hotel room, he was thinking about everything that had happened that day.

When the limousine arrived at the hospital earlier that day and they'd been surrounded by doctors, nurses and policemen all shouting and issuing directions he'd managed to slip away and hopped on a bus back to the hotel. It had been easy. He smiled to himself, it had been like the old days when he thrived on adrenalin, although, he admitted to himself as he unconsciously patted his stomach, he was a good bit slimmer and fitter in those days and would probably have jogged back to the hotel rather than have caught a bus.

Vincent had been keeping him updated throughout the day. Apparently Holly was going to be okay and Schultz was genuinely pleased about that, he liked her, she had spunk and the memory of her taking out that Sylvia woman would make him grin for a long time to come. Vincent told him that she'd spoken at length with the police, then slept soundly throughout the afternoon before waking up and announcing she'd like to talk about the land tomorrow, she knew what she wanted to do apparently and somehow, Schultz was not surprised. Vincent also mentioned that he'd had cawfee with DI Drummond and although Drummond had asked him a few difficult questions there had been nothing he couldn't answer.

Schultz felt calm despite the fact he wasn't certain whether or not Holly could identify him, he'd just continue to do his job as best he could until the very end. Which may, he mused as he gulped down his cold beer, happen a lot sooner than originally planned.

Max Henderson was just over half way across the Atlantic in his private jet and was also sitting in a comfortable armchair. He hadn't had to undo any buttons although he was considering a beer. He was calculating what to do next; he clicked his neck sharply to one side as he thought. He was already aware a link had been made that could connect Schultz, and therefore Ladyluck Corporation, to the murder of Mark Sharpe.

He, Max, had miscalculated, something he'd admit only to himself. He should not have ordered the killing with immediate effect but waited until after the deal was done, he'd risked putting a very real doubt in the minds of the government officials that he was something other than a powerful and wealthy businessman. Ladyluck had to be whiter than white. It was his error and one he should not have made.

But Schultz, what to do with Schultz – had the girl seen him or not? That was the key...

Drummond got off the phone to his wife with a wistful look in his dark eyes, he missed her and was looking forward to going home. How she put up with his job and his hours, his obsessiveness with a case, he'd never know and he thanked his lucky stars that he had her – she was smart, intelligent and blessed with the patience of a saint and quite why she'd chosen him was something he'd never quite figured out.

She'd been so pleased that Holly had been found alive but was even more pleased that he'd be home in good time for Christmas. He grinned, she probably had a Christmas shopping list as long as his arm all ready and waiting for him. But for now, even though it had already been a long day, he settled down at a borrowed desk with Axler sitting opposite, and started to sort through the massive pile of forms that came with working on two attempted murders, one murder and one suspected murder.

He tapped the desktop with his pen as he thought of Mark Sharpe – the man was obviously an unpleasant individual but he hadn't deserved to be killed in that way. He had a gut feeling that Schultz, the man in the car, was implicated but no evidence had come to light and he knew there was no point in trying to get a search warrant based on his gut, although he wished it was that easy, his gut was usually pretty accurate.

When he'd questioned Vincent Merino over coffee, Vincent had been courteous and stuck to the facts - yes, Schultz had arrived the previous day in a private jet owned by Ladyluck, he'd checked into the hotel in Chelmsford with himself and O'Malley and had stayed there all day going over papers and yes, Schultz had visited the land with them the next morning. He hadn't made himself known because there had been no need and he'd made his way back to the hotel from the hospital because he hadn't wanted to make a fuss - Holly's welfare had been uppermost in his mind. Unfortunately for Drummond, not wanting to make your presence known was not a crime. So they had nothing to go on - so far anyway, Drummond was nothing if not tenacious and would continue his investigation. He rubbed his stubbled chin with the palm of his hand and settled down to form filling.

Despite the long days Axler wasn't tired, he was still energised, running on adrenalin; he'd learnt so much working with Drummond and was now determined to become a detective. He glanced at the pile of paperwork and inwardly groaned, the exciting bit was most definitely over. He pushed back his chair and went to get them each a cup of strong, black coffee, it was going to be a long night.

Mrs Langstone hummed as she did the washing up, pushing random curls back off her face with the back of her hand. She was planning the Christmas lunch. She was so happy that Holly had been found and the last couple of days had actually been rather exciting. She could have done without the worry of Georgie running off but, she considered as she scrubbed a saucepan, Georgie was a very sensible girl and wouldn't have got herself into any real harm, not really.

And she'd enjoyed having company as well, Mr McKay was so nice. She beamed at him as she handed him the saucepan to dry and he smiled back, feeling perfectly at home.

Henry was unhappy and sat in the living room his head hung low, his liquid brown eyes sad - no matter how hard he tried that other furry creature just did not want to be his friend. Domino opened an eye and glanced down at him from the back of the sofa. If a cat could raise its eyebrows then that's what he did. He yawned widely then jumped down, padded over to Henry and started to roughly wash his face. Henry's tail wagged happily and then he peed on the carpet with excitement.

Jon was quiet but his fingers drummed the arm of the settee restlessly. The television was on but he wasn't watching it.

They'd all gone to the station as Drummond had asked and both he and Georgie had made a full statement before going on to see Holly. He frowned as he went over his conversation with Drummond. He was fully aware just how lucky he'd been; Drummond had been severe with him asking, no, demanding that Jon come and see him on a regular basis so he could keep a personal eye on him, but no formal charges had been made.

His father had found a quiet five minutes to give him a roasting that had been like no other and to inform him that his punishment would be decided after Christmas and that Jon could be assured it would be something pretty horrific. But he'd then hugged him and told him he was proud of him – parents, go figure.

# UNLUCKY DIP

Jon thought of Holly and all that she'd been through and he felt incredibly sad. Although the experience of the last few days had had a profound effect on him he knew he'd basically go back to his old life whereas Holly's life would never be the same again and she still had so much to face. They'd give her as much support as they could and maybe, he glanced down, maybe he'd even consider buying a new t-shirt that didn't have Iron Maiden on it...

Georgie was in her bedroom, making plans for when Holly came to live with them. Her mum had agreed that turning the small bedroom into Holly's room could be her project and she had a ton of ideas about how to make it special for her arrival. She thumbed through the photograph albums and she came across a picture taken at Holly's tenth birthday, Mr Maddon had his arms around both of them – his girls he called them. An immense sense of loss hit her, taking her breath away and sobs racked her body. There was a brief knock on her door and Jon came in. Without saying anything he sat on the edge of her bed, reached over, pulled a couple of tissues from a box and handed them to her and once she'd wiped her eyes and blown her nose they looked through the album together.

Vincent stared out of the car window on his way back to the hotel. Holly was already settled in the best private hospital around, he'd ensured that a low profile but efficient guard was kept on her and that she was comfortable. He started to relax, he'd have something to eat with Schultz, then tomorrow they'd both meet with Mr Henderson to update him and take it from there. He wondered if he'd have time to do some Christmas shopping in London for his gyrls, he hoped so, and maybe he'd even get some of his special cawfee sent to Drummond... yeah, he'd do that.

Sylvia sat on the edge of the metal bed in her cell

angry and upset, there wasn't a mirror in the place and she needed a change of clothes. Much to her disgust, the doctor had declared her fit and well. She'd been drugged – how could she be well? Why wasn't she in a hospital bed being looked after properly? She looked down in despair at her broken nails – not one person here would agree to her even having an emery board, how on earth did they expect her to manage? She turned around banged wildly on the wall with her metal mug hoping to disturb David Sharpe who was in the next cell. "This is all your fault!" she screamed at him.

Sharpe was lying down on his bed, looking up at the ceiling and raised his eyebrows at her outburst, stupid woman he thought, and continued trying to work out how he was going to defend himself in court. He was sure he could convince the jury that he was an upstanding member of the community and had been drawn into these unpleasant events unwittingly. He was so sure of his abilities that he'd decided to defend himself and imagined himself striding around the courtroom, magically drawing the jury into his world. He smiled to himself as he lay there, completely oblivious to the continued insults hurled at him from the next cell.

Holly was in bed, propped up by a mountain of pillows. A television was on in one corner but the sound was down low and she was alone for the first time that day – no police, no friends, no minders, no nurses or doctors. At that moment, however, she could have been anywhere because for her the room didn't exist - weariness and immense bleak sadness for everything she had lost swept over her like a tidal wave. She closed her eyes and sank down into darkness. As she floated downwards she heard a familiar voice say, "hold my hand Holly" and instinctively she reached out. A firm hand took hers and she opened her eyes to see her father.  He looked at her and smiled, his grey eyes crinkled at the corners.  "Holly," he said.

Her heart leapt and she threw her arms around him.  "Dad!!"

"I'm here to make sure you don't fall any further," he said, holding her tightly.

Holly looked around for the first time and realised they were both standing at the edge of a sheer cliff.  "Your path," said her father, "might be one which is less travelled than most, but you really don't want to head in that direction."  He pointed into the abyss.

Holly looked up at him, her eyes bright with tears.  "Can I stay here with you?  I don't want to go back, I miss you so much, I just feel... my heart..."  Words could not express the immense pain she felt.

Her father smoothed her hair.  "I miss you so much as well and I'm so proud of you Holly but you can't say here, you have a wonderful life ahead of you and you shouldn't miss a minute of it."

Her heart sank, her limbs felt heavy, useless.  "Can I stay for a little bit then?  Please?  It's been so hard without you..."

Her father smiled and nodded.  "I think that's allowed, let's sit down shall we?  Away from the edge would be good."

They walked a few steps away and sat on soft grass; Holly leant against him and he put an arm around her shoulders.  "Nothing will ever be the same will it?" she asked.

"No, it won't," her father's voice was gentle, "but that doesn't mean it will be bad."

"You won't be with me though."

"I love you Holly, I'll always be with you, don't ever doubt it."

"And during the good times as well?  There *will* be good times won't there?"

Her father laughed softly and hugged her.  "Your life will be full of good times and I'll be with you always, forever Holly."

# UNLUCKY DIP

She leant her head against his shoulder and for the first time for a long, long time closed her eyes in peaceful sleep.

# UNLUCKY DIP

## SEVEN MONTHS LATER

Schultz was sitting on his veranda with a beer in one hand watching the sun set over the Miami horizon. He loved this time of day, the sea was a kaleidoscope of colour, sometimes brilliant sometimes subtle but always steadfastly beautiful. He heard a car pull up and then the door slam. Footsteps headed in his direction across the gravel making crunching noises. A familiar head popped around the corner. "Hey Schultz, old buddy, how you doing?"

Schultz sat up in surprise. "Hey Vinny, how are you? Come and have a beer with me, you must have had a long journey – you down for long?"

"Nah, just this evening," replied Vinny, swigging back the beer and loosening his tie. "This is a great place you got here," he let out a long, low whistle. "That's sure some view – don't get nothing like that in New Yawk, mind you, there ain't hardly much sky t'see there..."

There was a long pause as they both contemplated the sunset.

"Just wait until the sun goes down will you Vin?" asked Schultz quietly.

Vin put down the bottle, a ring of cold water appeared immediately on the table. "Sure thing. And I'm sorry about having to do this but it ain't going away – that cop Drummond's like a bulldog you know, he's still rattling cages, he ain't never going to stop."

Schultz nodded appreciatively. "Yeah, he's a decent cop, didn't really expect nothing else."

They continued to watch the sun slowly descend.

"Make sure Gina doesn't see anything won't you Vin?" asked Schultz.

"Rely on me Schultz, I'll take care of her like she was a princess and Mr Henderson'll make sure she don't want for nothing."

Apart from me thought Schultz. Apart from me.

And he and Vinny sat watching the beauty of the sunset until finally there was no colour left, only darkness.

Even though she was expecting it, the sharp explosion of the champagne cork startled Holly. Loud cheering and thunderous applause filled the marquee and she watched Max Henderson doing what he did best, charming his wealthy and influential guests at the official opening of the construction of Casino City. He took a spade that looked like silver it had been polished so much and, with much ceremony, dug it firmly into the ground and turned over the first spadeful of thick earth. Beautiful showgirls with long legs and sparkling costumes posed either side of him. Cameras clicked, lights flashed and guests smiled broadly. If everything went according to plan then in just over a year the UK's first glittering Las Vegas style casino set in tastefully landscaped English countryside would be open to the public. Holly turned to Georgie who was standing next to her, beaming face upturned, loving every second of the drama and excitement of the event. "I'm just going to go get some fresh air, I won't be long," she said.

"You okay?" Georgie was immediately concerned.

Holly touched Georgie's arm briefly. "I'm fine, it's just very hot in here – probably that Buck's Fizz I drank earlier."

"I'll find you in a few minutes – ooh!" Another champagne cork went flying. "Can you believe the amount of alcohol he's wasting – scandalous!"

Holly exited quietly, weaving her way through the expensively dressed audience, and made her way out to the countryside beyond. She found a table surrounded by comfortable chairs and looked back at the grand marque. The muffled sounds of music and people talking and laughing floated through the air and she relaxed, thinking about everything that happened over the past few months.

# UNLUCKY DIP

Max Henderson had arrived in quiet style at the hospital to see her. From the background checks that she and Jon had done she'd known he was a formidable character but in hindsight she was pleased she hadn't known exactly how formidable. It had been like having a tiger in the room, on the surface he was pleasant, watchful and polite but she knew that on the inside he was restlessly prowling to and fro.

She'd kept her cool, however, and tucked up in bed, had negotiated the deal she wanted. She would not, she explained, sell the land to him, her father had died because of it and she wouldn't change her mind. His face hadn't flickered when she'd told him this, but remained perfectly composed. However, she'd gone on to say, she didn't see why he couldn't have full right of access across it but there would be conditions attached, for one thing, a full survey had to be done to ensure the road was laid in way that ensured the impact on the land and the wildlife was minimal. She was sure, she told him, he would get some good publicity out of being environmentally conscious and he nodded his agreement. She asked that an avenue of trees run along the length of the road and that the land on either side be properly maintained so that it would become a sanctuary for local wildlife.

When he asked if she wanted payment or any other kind of financial recompense for allowing him access she shook her head in a decisive no, she wouldn't take money. It was money and greed that had led to her father's death and to two attempts on her life and she was simply not interested - she wanted nothing other than the conditions she'd asked for.

Max Henderson had sat back in the chair next to her hospital bed studying this young girl with the steady grey eyes and pretty heart shaped face. Vincent had briefed him earlier, telling him she was remarkable and he hadn't exaggerated; Max knew she was absolutely genuine in what she said. Wanting control, power and money because she had something she knew he needed was not on her agenda. Although he wasn't used to dealing with people like Holly, he did not deride or underestimate her simply because she didn't want the same things he did, he appreciated and valued her feelings of loyalty to her father and her honesty.

Her offer, however, put him in a quandary because although he knew he was getting a remarkable deal he didn't enjoy getting something for nothing and neither did he like the uncomfortable feeling he was beholden to someone. And, of course, the land he wanted would not be his, something that went against the grain but he knew she would be intractable and so he accepted gracefully – maybe, he thought, an opportunity would come up at a later date.

He'd leant back in the chair as he thought through her terms, cricked his neck to one side and asked if she would accept a gift from him? He'd like to establish a trust which would provide scholarships for budding architects. The scholarships would be granted in her father's name and awarded annually. Holly was a little shaken at this suggestion but then beamed and said yes, that would suit her fine. Henderson stood up and shook her hand, it was a deal, he'd get his lawyers to speak to her lawyers. And then he left leaving Holly in a state of panic because she didn't have any lawyers.

Now, what had been a mere dream was now becoming a reality.

The air cooled and Holly breathed it in deeply, grateful to be out in the open. Max Henderson had been as good as his word and had taken care of everything in a fair and honest manner. Her land had been carefully developed and maintained and he gave generous donations to local wildlife centres to help ease any impact the casino may have on the environment. He'd also established a scholarship trust as promised and students were already applying for awards. The last few months had been difficult, painful, as she'd tried to come to terms with what had happened and adjust to her new life with Georgie, her mum and Henry but all the boxes containing all her memories were delivered from the flat in Kensington and she finally unpacked them, making as much mess as she wanted, and that certainly helped.

Jon and his father drove up to see them regularly. Jon, Georgie and Holly watched, first with surprise and then with keen interest as romance blossomed between Georgie's mum and Jon's father. Jon protested loudly that the possibility of gaining two extra sisters on top of the one he already had was way too much for him to handle and that he'd seriously have to think about emigrating but was shouted down by the two girls who thought it was all very romantic. The three of them grew very close, partly because everything that had happened and everything that they still had to endure – court appearances, lawyers, statements, constant bombardment from the press. There was a big gap in Holly's life and at first was almost grateful for all the activity and distraction but as things settled down she felt its presence more like a permanent ache in her heart.

Holly became aware that the music had been turned up a notch in the background and realised that the speeches must now be over and the party beginning. She leant forward, her elbows on the table, taking in the beautiful surroundings, so serene against the loud music. She grimaced as she thought of Sylvia. The case was still on-going, mostly because the psychiatrists couldn't make out if she was sane or not, but it did look fairly certain she'd languish, complaining, in a prison for the rest of her life. David Sharpe's case had already been heard and he'd lost everything despite his absolute conviction that he was going to be vindicated. He'd be in prison for many years to come. Holly didn't feel any pity for either of them, she was only sorry she didn't get the chance to deck David Sharpe as well while she had the chance.

As for the person who had shot Mark, well, that would always be a mystery but she knew that Drummond was still working on the case and would never lose sight of it.

She heard a movement to one side and turned around, Jon was standing there, rocking back on his heels, hands in pockets. He looked, she noted, surprisingly handsome for a computer geek. He'd changed recently especially since he'd finished his exams at college; he was taller, his shoulders had broadened out and she and Georgie had taken him on a few shopping trips to teach him some fashion basics. The infamous Iron Maiden t-shirt had long since been relegated to the recycling bin.

"Holly?" His eyes didn't miss anything in their quick check to see if she was really alright. She was very composed but then, he thought, she always was. "Are you okay?"

Georgie strode up quickly behind him. "Aha! And why are you lurking out here? You know how nervous I get when you disappear at parties."

Holly laughed and pulled a face. "You don't have to worry, there's no water around here unless you count the chocolate fountains and I'd happily dive into those! Nah, I just needed some fresh air, there are way too many people in there for me."

Jon pulled up a couple of chairs, one for Georgie and one for himself and they sat either side of her. "Hey, did either of you see Drummond in there?" he asked.

Georgie giggled. "That's the first time I've seen him without his raincoat on. He looked dead uncomfortable, like a snail without its shell. Was PC Axler there? He's soooo gorgeous, I wouldn't mind seeing him all done up."

"Georgie, you're a lost cause!" laughed Holly. "Mind you, I have to agree, he's not bad – how many? 8 or 9 do you reckon?"

# UNLUCKY DIP

Jon rolled his eyes. "Excuse me, how old are you two and there is a man present."

Georgie looked around. "Where?" she asked.

"Oh very funny."

"I suppose," Holly blew out a sigh, "we'd better get back at some point and show our faces."

"They're about to open the buffet as well," pointed out Georgie.

"But it's nice out here," said Jon. "Away from the maddening crowd and all that."

"The showgirls are apparently serving the buffet," tempted Georgie.

"Like right," he replied, "and risk getting their feathers and tassels in a dip? I don't think so somehow."

Holly giggled. Dusk was falling and lingering shafts of white light sparkled like sharp diamonds in the sky and she gave a small sigh of contentment. Jon reached across, took her hand and squeezed it reassuringly. Holly glanced across at him and smiled, everything was going to be alright.